POISON PEN

Patty left with the book, and I returned to the mail. There it was, at the bottom of the pile: a letter for me with no return address. I stared at it for a heartbeat, then two. Through the thick white envelope, I felt its contents growl. This was bad. I squeezed my fingers into fists and released them and fumbled for the letter opener.

Unlike the other letters, mine was written by hand— no glued-on words cut from magazines. Its message was simple, in black ink: *I know your secret.* That was all.

I stood, the letter dangling from my fingers. Who wrote this? The secret it mentioned—did someone know I was a witch? My breath came quickly.

Rodney hopped to the desk and, hackles raised, backed away from the letter. He hissed and jumped to the floor.

Books by Angela M. Sanders

BAIT AND WITCH

SEVEN-YEAR WITCH

WITCH AND FAMOUS

WITCH UPON A STAR

GONE WITH THE WITCH

THE WITCH IS BACK

Published by Kensington Publishing Corp.

The
Witch Is
Back

Angela M. Sanders

Kensington Publishing Corp.
www.kensingtonbooks.com

First Printing: December 2024
ISBN: 978-1-4967-4095-3

ISBN: 978-1-4967-4096-0 (ebook)

10 9 8 7 6 5 4 3 2 1

Printed in the United States of America

The
Witch Is
Back

CHAPTER ONE

"Mom," I said, "Please tell me what's wrong."

"I don't know what you're talking about," my mother replied in a chipper tone. She was sore about something, all right.

I cranked down the car window to a hot breeze smelling of pine needles. "I love seeing you. But to show up unexpected? That's not like you."

What else wasn't like my mother was how quiet she was. Normally Mom would have circled my apartment on the top floor of Wilfred's library with a pad of paper in hand, listing the various ways I could improve my life: More sprouts in the refrigerator; make sure my cat Rodney's food was high protein; and don't forget to separate the whites from darks when doing laundry. Instead, she lounged on the couch with a vacant look in her eyes—except for the half hour she'd spent furiously reorganizing my silverware drawer.

She was also cagey about how long she planned to stay. Granted, it had been barely a day since I'd picked her up at the airport, but I didn't have to be a witch to know something was on her mind.

"Can't I visit my daughter without an excuse?" was all she'd say.

I couldn't force her to talk, but I could distract her with a visit to an estate sale all of Wilfred had anticipated for weeks, ever since Reverend Clarence Duffy's death. Reverend Duffy had shut himself up at home for the past two decades with only his son Adam to care for him. He was a mysterious figure, and the opportunity to peek into his life through his belongings was the weekend's chief entertainment.

I pulled my old Corolla onto the highway that led out of Wilfred. The road ended three miles later at Marlin Hill, a long-abandoned town built on a collection of steep hills. A few decrepit houses, roofs heavy with moss, clung to its fir-blanketed hillsides, giving it the air of a stage set for a horror movie. Cicadas chirped in the heat. The town's church, a whitewashed wooden chapel, had survived, however, and so did its former pastor's home, where we were now headed.

We parked along a rutted dirt road and walked to the house. Cars lined the drive. I wasn't sure what I was expecting, but it wasn't this modernist beauty, constructed at angles and cantilevered over the hill.

"Look, Mom." I sheltered my eyes from the sun and pointed. "Isn't it magnificent? No wonder they call it the Aerie."

Mom, still in a foul mood, pulled a fluff of moss from the window next to the house's entry. "Looks like it could use some maintenance."

There was no denying the house had seen better days. Oregon's famously damp winters had rotted its windowsills here and there, and the cedar siding could have used a fresh coat of varnish. But the house loomed above Marlin Hill like the manor on the cover of a paperback gothic romance—if it had been designed by the father in *The Brady Bunch*, that is.

"I love it. It could be a feature in a 1970s issue of *Architectural Digest*."

From behind us came a voice. "My thought exactly."

We turned to see a stranger approaching from a path emerging from the woods. He wore a white linen suit that would have been more at home in Old Havana than in Oregon, but with his easy posture—hands in pockets—and feline grace, somehow it worked. He lifted his nose to breathe the summer air.

"But it was built a decade later. A late example of the Pacific Northwest regional style," the stranger said. At our surprised glance, he added, "My father was an architect. Such a lovely property. Quiet."

I was surprised I hadn't already caught wind of the stranger's presence. Wilfred was so small and the grapevine so robust that you couldn't burn toast without hearing about it the next time you bought margarine. "I don't believe we've met. I'm Josie Way, and this is my mother, Nora."

"Emilio Landau." A small green and gold embroidered eel, complete with fangs, adorned his jacket pocket. He noted my glance. "Emilio E. Landau, that is. E.E.L. My emblem."

I couldn't help but dig for more information. It

would be a hot commodity later, down at the café, and I rarely had the jump on Wilfred old-timers Patty and Darla for gathering intelligence. "A friend of the reverend?"

"Dear me, no. Simply visiting these parts."

Evasive. I tried again. "You must be here for the"— I wrinkled my nose, trying to recall what workshop the retreat center was hosting—"yodeling camp?" There was little other reason to stay in Wilfred longer than the few hours it took to have breakfast at Darla's Café and peruse the This-N-That.

He laughed soundlessly, like Charles Boyer in a silent film. "No. Simply looking around, enjoying country life." He extracted a business card from a silver case. I caught only a glance of his name, his signature eel, and "art appraiser" before my mother deftly extracted it from his fingertips.

Emilio Landau disappeared up the drive as if he were strolling La Croisette in Cannes, taking in a Mediterranean sunset instead of dodging blackberry vines on a dusty dirt road.

Mom watched him walk away. I had to nudge her arm to get her attention. Given her mood, I was glad to see her intrigued about something.

We stepped into a low-ceilinged entry hall with shabby carpet that made the main room, when we entered, all the more glorious. "Oh, my," Mom said.

Floor-to-ceiling windows stretched two stories high. Instead of browsing the tagged furniture and the case of jewelry near the cash register in the living room, we were both drawn across the house to the view.

I greeted Adam, Reverend Duffy's son. Adam taught music at the high school and occasionally played the mandolin in a country music ensemble in Forest Grove, Wilfred's bigger city neighbor, and with his neat beard and short-sleeved western shirt, he looked the part. When Adam stopped by the library, which wasn't often, the books, making suggestions only my witch's ears could hear, were desperate for him to take a vacation from caring for his father and offered up travel guides to beach locales.

I introduced Adam to my mother. He slid open the door to the deck. "Come outside. You've never seen anything like it. Plus, I'd like you to meet my brother, Benjamin, and his wife Lucy. They're here from New York."

Outside, the breeze ruffled our hair. As Adam had promised, the view was stupendous. The rise on which the Aerie was built dropped precipitously, opening to a view to the valley backed by faraway mountains cloaked with lush green conifers. Two weathered wooden chairs sat on the deck, one of them holding a guitar and a mandolin. Apparently the Duffy brothers were both musicians.

"Sunrises must be breathtaking," I said.

"Unmatchable," said Benjamin. He might have been a younger, more cheerful version of his brother, with dark shaggy hair and a gap-toothed smile that made me smile, too.

"It's busy here," Mom said.

"We're glad to see it," Lucy said.

Benjamin lifted the guitar next to him. "I won't lie.

The income from the sale will come in handy." He picked out a song that might have been written a century earlier, a tune that tugged at my memory.

Adam joined him on the mandolin, and their voices harmonized. Now I knew it. It was the old gospel tune, "I'll Fly Away."

"Talented," Mom whispered.

I fought the urge to sing along. "Definitely."

As the music drifted through the house, people nudged their way to the deck to listen. One man tapped a windowsill in time.

The gathering audience seemed to trigger something in Adam. He lifted the guitar from his brother's hands. "This doesn't feel right. Not now. Not so soon after Dad died."

Benjamin's smile faded abruptly. He turned his head toward the faraway mountains.

Lucy, Benjamin's wife, watched the interaction with an expression I couldn't read. A tattoo of a rose with black-green thorns wound up her bare shoulder, its stem tucked somewhere inside the halter of her sundress. Her sleek black hair was coiled into a braided bun. Whatever she was feeling, it wasn't a surfeit of joy.

Absorbed by the view, Mom seemed oblivious to the interaction I'd just witnessed between Adam and Benjamin. What was on her mind? She stepped forward to grasp the railing, but Benjamin quickly blocked her with an arm. "Watch that. I wouldn't trust the handrail. The house needs a lot of work." He pulled at the railing to show its wobble. "It's top of the list of repairs."

Mom backed off and joined me. A hawk circled above the house, riding a current of warm air. "It's so nice to be home," Benjamin said. "I'd forgotten how beautiful it is here." He slipped an arm around his wife's shoulders. "We're both looking forward to settling in."

Lucy flashed a dim smile. "I'm going into the house for a glass of water. It's hot out here."

We followed Lucy inside and joined the dozen or so people wandering the estate sale.

Our first stop was upstairs, the bedrooms. In what must have been the reverend's room, at the back of the house with the view, was a couple opening a colonial-style dresser's drawers and measuring its length. Folded linens were stacked on the bed, and the open closet showed frayed plaid shirts. Despite the light and open view, the room felt oppressive. I imagined the reverend's last weeks in bed. A bell still rested on the nightstand. Had he rung that bell for Adam to bring him lunch, his pills, take him to the bathroom?

"Let's move on," I suggested to Mom. Maybe the rest of the house would be more cheerful.

From the hall rose a staircase to the third floor, but it was roped off, and a door on the landing above closed it off from the rest of the house. Books upstairs called to me. I sensed romance and mystery novels, long unread and lonely.

"Mother's suite," Adam said. I hadn't known he was behind us. "Dad wanted it kept as it was when she died. Maybe we'll open it up now. It's been a long time."

We retraced our steps downstairs. On the ground

floor, to the left of the entryway, was what must have been Reverend Duffy's office. A heavy mahogany desk with lions' heads carved on its legs loomed like a battleship in the room's center. It was bare, but for a green glass-shaded lamp. But what attracted my attention were the crates, already tagged SOLD, stacked against the opposite wall. Before I entered the room I'd felt their energy. Here were books, scores of them, and they chilled my blood. The books hissed and grumbled, chanting warnings and whispering hellfire. Whoever the reverend was, whatever he'd become, I didn't like it. I backed out of the room.

Mom grabbed my hand. "Honey, let's get out of here."

I was the more powerful witch, but Mom had the gift of foresight, which, due to her reluctance to embrace magic, rarely showed itself. Apparently it showed itself now.

"We haven't even seen the kitchen," I said.

"Seriously, let's leave."

We waved our goodbyes, and from the dining room, Benjamin returned a wave. Lucy and Adam had disappeared. Mom grabbed my arm and hustled me into the summer afternoon.

Back in the car, I turned to her. "You felt it, too?"

She settled into the passenger seat and stared straight ahead through the windshield. "I don't know what I feel anymore."

I started the car and eased down the steep driveway, more to get air circulating through its open windows than to return home. I didn't have air conditioning. "What do you mean?"

"Oh, honey."

"You felt that bad vibe from the house, too, didn't you?" Now we were on the narrow road that led from Marlin Hill, and the afternoon's stuffiness dissipated.

"Josie, I need to tell you something." Mom repositioned her purse on her lap and drew a deep breath. "Your father and I are getting a divorce."

CHAPTER TWO

Divorce? My mother must be joking. "You said what?"

She sat resolute in the passenger seat, lips firmly sealed. I knew that look. She'd told me all she was going to—for the moment, at least.

I had certainly not sensed trouble between my parents. My father, a community college professor, seemed happy researching the breakfast habits of Louis XV or exploring some other obscure corner of French history. When he wasn't at the college, he was usually parked in an armchair in his cluttered office with half-empty coffee cups and stacks of papers around him. The term "absent-minded professor" might have been coined for him. That said, he was a kindhearted man, and he would do anything to help his daughters—if he lifted his nose from a book long enough to notice something was wrong.

My mother ran the house, making sure dinner was on the table, the lawn was mowed, and property taxes were paid. She was also a successful real estate agent known for driving a hard bargain. On the face of it, my parents were as different as gin and milk, but seeing the love in my father's eyes as he surfaced from his studies when my mother called him to the table, or the tender care Mom took in bleaching ink stains from Dad's shirts, was proof of their bond.

And now my mother tells me they're getting a divorce.

When we arrived home at the library, Mom continued to keep silent. We mounted the steps to my rooms on the library's third floor, an apartment carved from the servants' quarters from when the library was Thurston Wilfred's mansion.

"Mom, aren't you going to say anything? You can't drop a bombshell like that without telling me more."

"What, dear?" She plastered a smile on her face.

I could only sigh. I dropped my purse in the living room beneath a gold-framed mirror and froze. The hairs on my neck prickled. In the mirror's reflection were the trees outside the window opposite, the grandmotherly angles of my worn Victorian sofa, and my mother, with a puzzled expression. There was no me. I was not reflected in the mirror.

"Josie?" Mom said.

My reflection slowly materialized, my expression twice as puzzled as my mother's. What had I just seen—or not seen?

"Josie," Mom repeated. "What's wrong?"

"Nothing." This was not the first time something eerie like this had happened in recent months, but I didn't want to alarm Mom. After all, these occurrences, strange as they were, had been harmless. I drew a fresh breath. "Lyndon should have set up the bed for you by now. Are you sure you want to sleep way, way over in the tower room? I can sleep on the couch, and you take my bed."

Down the hall from my apartment was the door leading to a semi-sheltered room formed by the Italianate tower rising from the Victorian mansion's face. The door was propped open now, and I led my mother toward it. Sure enough, a twin bed was set up in the corner, and Lyndon, the library's caretaker, had even been thoughtful enough to bring in a side table and lamp. The floor was neatly swept.

"It will be perfect," Mom said. "I don't want you sleeping on the couch while I'm here, and besides, I need space of my own to think."

My cat, Rodney, swaggered in and jumped on the bed, making himself at home on my mother's pillow. My gaze shot to Mom, but she didn't even seem to notice. She wandered to the open windows and stared into the distance while the firs swished in the breeze.

She turned to me. "I have no purpose anymore."

"What do you mean?"

Rodney, a circle of black fur on Mom's white pillow, raised his head.

"You girls are grown up now. Toni has a family, and her medical practice is doing well. You seem to have found a good place for yourself." She laid a hand on my shoulder. "You look good, Josie. Happy. I can't wait to meet Sam."

I might have glowed just a bit more. We had plans to

join Sam at the café that evening. "He wants to meet you, too."

"Even Jean is a success."

We'd all been worried about my baby sister, Jean. She had a talent for getting herself into pickles, but she'd established herself as a wellness coach and had enough clients that she could rent both an office and an apartment with an actual bedroom. She was even talking of holding a yoga retreat in Costa Rica.

"What does that have to do with you and Dad?" I asked.

Mom sat on the bed, and Rodney left his cozy perch on her pillow to pad to her lap. Mom absently dropped a palm to his back. "I don't think your father even notices I'm alive."

"Mom!"

"I'm serious. I wouldn't be surprised if he hasn't figured out yet that I'm not home. He probably thinks I'm in the den watching TV."

I sat next to her on the bed. "That's crazy talk. Dad loves you. You don't know what you're saying."

"All he cares about is his work. As long as he has clean underwear and breakfast, he's happy. And I'm not even sure he'd miss those as long as he had a stack of eighteenth-century Breton birth records to annotate."

"That can't be true," I said. "He loves you."

"He might love me in his own way, but he lives for his work. I might as well not be there." She fidgeted with the sheet's edge. "A few weeks ago I told him I was off to visit your sister and he'd need to get his own dinner. He just grunted. So I told him I would be square-dancing with goats all night long. Thought I'd see if he was paying attention. What did he do?"

"What?" I said, although I suspected I knew.

"Nothing. He grunted again. Then I mentioned the goats were under the care of Charlemagne. That got his attention."

"What did he do then?"

"He said something in French. I didn't bother replying, even if I could."

I got it. Dad could translate old French documents, but he had a horrible accent when speaking. The one time we'd made a family trip to Paris, Dad had somehow accidentally convinced the tour guide I was vegan. I never ate so much leek soup in my life.

The cross breeze through the tower's windows rippled the linen tablecloths strung up as makeshift curtains. Rodney moved so he could sit in Mom's lap and rest his head in mine.

"Your father doesn't understand me. Worse, I don't think he cares."

This couldn't be true. Dad might have taken her for granted, but surely he cared. "Maybe he feels you have your own thing going on, you know, with being a witch and all."

Mom never talked about her magic, and she'd outright refused to tell me about mine until it had made itself known despite her best efforts to suppress it. My magic was much stronger than my mother's or that of my two sisters, who were healers, but we all came from a magical bloodline.

I wouldn't be surprised if many people had magic of

my mother's magnitude and hadn't even tuned into it. Mona's gift with animals was a sort of magic, for instance. Darla knew food, and people drove in for miles for her Pacific Northwestern take on Southern standards. Patty could find fascinating objects anywhere for her shop. All magic.

"Hmm," Mom said. She tilted her head. "Have you told Sam about your abilities?"

I waited, as if an answer other than yes or no would occur to me. It didn't. "No."

"My magic is one thing, honey, but yours is serious." Mom's voice raised in pitch. "Jean told me a few of the things she saw you do. Novels flying across the room. Books actually telling you things." She hooked a finger under Rodney's chin and tilted it up. "She said you can go into your cat's body."

Rodney, unperturbed, purred.

"That's all true." Wait—didn't we start out talking about Mom, not me?

Mom, once again chipper, fluffed her pillow. "I'm thinking a nap would be perfect about now. See you later."

I couldn't get to my phone fast enough. I closed the door between my living room and the hall overlooking the atrium, then for good measure shut myself into my adjoining bedroom.

Toni picked up on the third ring. "Josie? Is something wrong? Just a sec." A pause. "Letty, honey, we eat soup with a spoon, not our hands."

One thing about having sisters who were also witches

was that you didn't have to spend a lot of time on small talk. "Why didn't you tell me Mom and Dad are getting a divorce?"

"Is that all?"

"What do you mean, 'is that all'?" I said. "This is a big deal."

"Nonsense. Mom's been talking like this for months. What, did she call and complain that Dad forgot their anniversary again? Letty, dear. The spoon, not the fork."

Letty, my toddler niece, was a creative eater. A kid couldn't get in too much trouble eating soup with a fork, though. "Call? No, Mom's here. In Wilfred. She telephoned last night from the airport and told me to come get her."

"She's in Oregon with you?"

"Yes. She's taking a nap down the hall."

"Dad must have really done something to set her off," Toni said.

We both pondered that for a moment. Dad wasn't the type to intentionally set anyone off. However, we could imagine how he might do it unintentionally.

"How long is she staying?" Toni asked.

"Don't know. She won't say. She brought only one suitcase."

"That doesn't mean anything."

I understood Toni instantly. Mom was a master of the capsule wardrobe transformed by accessories and had lectured us frequently over the years about the power of a good scarf to take you from day to evening. With a change of lipstick, heels, and a canny bolero, she might go from a soup kitchen volunteer shift to a dinner date. It was all part of her efficient approach to life.

"I still can't buy a purse without making sure it could hold an evening clutch," Toni added. "Even though these days I'm more likely to need wet wipes for Letty and scrubs for the hospital."

"So, you don't know what's going on with her, either," I said.

"Let me call Dad and get back to you," Toni said. "I'm sure it's a simple misunderstanding."

CHAPTER THREE

That evening, the laughter and clinking of cutlery on plates on the patio at Darla's Café comforted me. I gazed across the tables to take in Wilfredians I'd come to know and love. Over there, Mrs. Garlington sat with an iced tea and notebook at her elbow and her husband with his own notebook next to her. She would be drafting a sonnet while he sketched butterflies. At the other end of the patio sat Duke and Desmond, arguing about gasoline- versus diesel-powered engines. Near them, Mona nursed a puppy with a bottle and ate bites of salad with her free hand.

In fact, I knew everyone at the diner that evening except a ferret-like man in an ironed button-up shirt sitting alone, awkwardly surveying the crowd. Maybe he was in town for the yodeling workshop at the retreat center, although he looked like he might better enjoy a seminar in spreadsheet management.

No matter what was happening between my parents,

at least I'd have Wilfred. And Sam. I glanced at my phone. Sam was late—not like him.

"In my day," Mom said, "when a man was about to meet his girlfriend's mother, he showed up on time."

"I don't understand. I confirmed with him." As soon as I'd picked up my mother at the airport, I'd made the date for the three of us—four, including baby Nicky— to have dinner together. It wasn't the first time Sam and I had crossed signals, either. Fortunately we had a strong enough relationship to laugh it off. I pulled out my phone and dialed Sam's number. He answered on the first ring. "Where are you?" I asked.

"What do you mean?" His voice acted on me like soothing music.

"My mom's in town and we arranged to have dinner together."

"Did we? I saw you had a guest, but I didn't want to intrude. It's your mother, you say?"

I checked my texts. Sure enough, the text I'd sent him hadn't gone through. Yet I was sure that not only had I made the date, he'd confirmed it. Strange. No matter—the important thing was that I had him on the phone now.

"If you're free, we're at the diner. Mom's looking forward to meeting you."

"I'll be right down. And, Josie, thank you for inviting me."

As I stowed my phone, I knew I smiled like I'd found a gold nugget in my purse. Sam had that effect on me.

Mom and I had barely received our glasses of iced

tea when Sam arrived, settling Nicky into a highchair and taking the seat next to mine. Nicky banged his palms on the tray, and his black curls bounced.

"I'm pleased to meet you, Ms. Way," Sam said.

Mom had been occupied with beaming at Nicky, and when she turned to focus on Sam, I watched her. Her real estate clients might not be able to read her moods, but to her daughters her moods showed as clearly as goldfish in an aquarium. I warmed as I observed her satisfaction, until her expression clouded. What did she see?

"Happy to meet you, too. Please call me Nora." Mom hadn't been confused by Sam's downturned lips. I'd explained his quirk of frowning when he was happy and smiling when upset. It was unusual, but like everything with Sam, I adored it. Mom picked up her menu. "Now, what should I order?"

When we all had platters of the daily special—jambalaya with local seafood—conversation turned from Sam's childhood in Wilfred to the goings-on in town today. "We went to the estate sale up at the Aerie this afternoon."

Sam fed Nicky a forkful of rice. "Reverend Duffy. I remember him from when I was a kid—I used to go to school with Adam. The reverend turned odd toward the end and spent his days cooped up in his office."

"What do you mean by 'odd'?" I asked.

"I don't know the details, just that at some point he withdrew from his pastorship, although he kept regular office hours at the church. Then there was Benjamin."

Patty would give me the rest of the story about the reverend if I asked. "What about him?"

"He was troubled. In and out of the juvenile justice system, and I think it really disturbed his father, who'd made a big thing of piety."

"Didn't used to be that way." Darla, the café's owner, had arrived with a water pitcher to refill our glasses. "You must be Josie's mother." Once introductions were completed, she continued. "Reverend Duffy was a gentle man. Reminded me more of how his son Adam is now. Always there if you needed a sympathetic ear. When his wife died, it all changed." A summons from across the patio drew Darla away.

Sam placed his hand over mine on the tabletop, which caught Mom's attention.

"Let me see that baby," Mom said. "Maybe he'd rather sit with me." She extricated him from his high chair, and Nicky gleefully swung into her lap.

"Is this your mother?" Lalena appeared at our table, with Ian not far behind her. Since the estate sale was over, apparently Mom had become Wilfred's greatest attraction. "I'm Lalena Dolby. I live back there." She waved a hand toward the Magnolia Rolling Estates, the trailer park Darla owned behind the café, where Lalena operated her business as a palm and tarot card reader with occasional forays into contacting the spirit world. I wondered what Mom thought of her outfit tonight, a lacy 1970s dress that would have made Stevie Nicks proud.

"Lalena's a good friend," I said. "And this is Ian Penclosa."

Ian rolled his wheelchair forward and proffered a hand. "Pleased to meet you."

Ian sold rare books in a stall at Patty's This-N-That,

although most of his business was online. I found him slightly disturbing, and I couldn't say why. Maybe it was his gruff expression, although he could unexpectedly break into a smile that was warm and even goofy. Maybe it was that he specialized in books on parapsychology. Or maybe it was the slice of scar that ran down one cheek. Whatever my assessment, Lalena had been gung-ho about him since they'd first met.

"Did you go to the estate sale at the Aerie today?" Lalena asked. "Ian and I were there when it opened. We bought crates of books, sight unseen."

I remembered the books hissing in Reverend Duffy's office. "How did you know they were worth buying?"

Lalena shrugged. "Ian talked with Adam. He said they'd brought them up from the church."

Ian wheeled his chair a foot closer. "The price was right. I sold a crate right away to the new guesthouse. Wallingford was looking for something to fill the library's shelves. The books have already paid for themselves."

"This is a social town," Mom observed. Nicky babbled on her lap as she bounced him. To anyone else, Mom was happily absorbed in dinner. I saw something else—some distraction. It must have been the specter of divorce. She and Dad were making a mistake. I knew it.

Ian and Lalena found a table at the patio's edge just as Buffy and Thor, Patty's grandchildren, showed up. Thor wore his signature cape and Buffy had on a sparkly pink skirt and tank top featuring a kitten in a basket. Thor set up a Bluetooth speaker. Buffy placed a box next to it ornamented with flowers scrawled in felt-tip marker.

"Ladies and gentlemen." Thor lifted the edge of his cape to mop his brow. "Please enjoy the spectacle of the Amazing Ellie. Your donations will be accepted here"—he pointed to Buffy's basket—"to pay for Ellie's majorette camp." He tapped on a tablet, and electronic dance music rose over the quickly diminishing conversation on the patio.

Ellie Wallingford, the thirteen-year-old daughter of the owners of the new Wallingford Guest House, emerged from behind a pickup truck in the parking lot and thrust a baton into the air. She stepped wide to the time of the music and caught the baton on its way down, twirling again to face the diners. She was good. Even Nicky was silent as Ellie's act intensified into an athletic mix of dance and whirling baton. To the side, Buffy aped her moves. Platters of burgers in hand, Darla emerged from the doorway that led to the kitchen.

"That girl knows what she's doing," Mom said.

"She does," Darla said. She'd slung a dishtowel over her shoulder and paused at our table to watch the show. "Too bad she can't stop telling stories."

Ellie deftly knelt and added a second baton to the routine. Their chromed shafts caught the early evening sun as they twirled overhead. I dipped into my purse for a donation.

"What do you mean by 'stories'?" Mom asked.

"The kid's a hound for attention. Yesterday morning she told me she'd been offered a starring role in a movie, but she had to turn it down because of school. Patty told me that Ellie tried to convince her she was in line for the British throne."

Then the inevitable happened. Just as Ellie had

added a third baton to the mix and the dance frenzy was coming to a climactic peak, she tripped on a pot-hole in the gravel parking lot. The batons spiraled into the patio, bouncing over tables. One hit the server's tray, dumping beer and an iced tea. Diners leapt to their feet as glasses shattered over the concrete floor.

Darla set the hamburgers on the nearest table and marched to Buffy and Thor. "Kids, get home. How many times have I told you to keep your moneymaking schemes out of the café? Do I have to call your grand-mother?" Since Darla and Patty were sisters, it was likely she'd hear about it, anyway. Darla cast a dirty look at Ellie, who stood defiant, arms crossed over her chest.

"Aunt Darla, we weren't in the café. We were in the parking lot," Buffy said in a wheedling tone.

"Get out of here. Go," Darla replied. Then, to the diners, "The show is over."

People stood, unclear whether to go or stay. Mrs. Garlington clutched her notebook, now soaked with tea, to her chest, and Mona protected the puppy with both arms.

"Why do I have to leave?" Ellie said. "I wasn't hurt-ing anyone. People liked it. Didn't you?"

None of us dared to respond and risk Darla's cen-sure. Sure, Ellie's show was entertaining, but, unlike Darla, she didn't serve the only dinner in town.

"I said to pack it up. Go," Darla said.

Ellie, showing she would take things at her own pace, slowly retrieved her batons and muttered some-thing under her breath. She stood straight and looked Darla in the eye before retreating, head high.

"Free scoops of homemade huckleberry ice cream to everyone on the patio," Darla added. Diners returned to their seats and conversation resumed.

A busboy was already sweeping up broken glass. Nicky crooned something unintelligible in a high note, and Mom tucked him back into the highchair.

Sam slipped an arm around my waist. I leaned into him. For the moment, I could ignore broken glass, disappointed kids, troubled books, and even my parents' divorce. I was happy.

Mom went in the library's side door first, giving me privacy to say goodnight to Sam.

"It was nice to meet your mother." Sam released Nicky, who waddled straight for Lyndon's cottage. Lyndon and Roz, the assistant librarian, would be living there for only a few more months until their house was finished being built. These days, Lyndon spent his spare hours planning its garden, but he always had a moment for Nicky.

"She likes you," I told Sam.

"How can you tell?" He placed his hands on both sides of my shoulders on the wall behind me, putting me in a Sam-trap, my favorite place.

"She asked you questions. She was open. She even gave you real estate advice." Despite my words, I remembered her clouded expression. She was getting some kind of hit off of him. What was it?

Sam kissed me. "I'm glad."

When the glow from his kiss subsided, I said, "There's one thing, though. She told me she and my father—"

Just then, a crow swooped from an oak tree and dove inches above Nicky's head. I gasped. Crows weren't supposed to be out after dark, and this wasn't the first time I'd seen them. In a flash, Sam had swept a crying Nicky into his arms.

"I'll leave you to put him to bed," I said. I could tell Sam about my parents' divorce later. "Good night."

Inside, Mom had already made her way to my apartment and stood in my kitchen removing the glasses from the cupboards.

"What are you doing?" I asked.

"You have them in the wrong place. They should be where the bowls are." She slid a stack of bowls from the adjacent cupboard. "You need to tell him."

I dropped to the chair at my tiny kitchen table. "Tell who what?"

"Tell Sam you're a witch. I didn't press the matter earlier, because I didn't know how serious you were about him. Now that I've seen you two together, the sooner you tell him, the better."

She wasn't saying anything I hadn't thought myself. I loved Sam and I had no intention of letting him go. However, keeping him meant complete honesty. If I told him I was a witch, would he think I'd lost my mind? Would he back away in fear? Would he even believe me?

Mom took the chair across from me, leaving a mess of bowls and tumblers crowding the sink. "Magic is too big a secret to keep between you."

"Was it hard to tell Dad? When you first saw him, you knew you were going to be together."

Mom averted her gaze. We'd heard the story over

and over of how she and my father had met, and I loved it every time. When she was barely twenty years old, Mom's car had broken down, and she was crossing the college's campus to find a phone when she ran into—literally—a student with his head down. "When I handed him the treatise on Talleyrand he'd dropped and looked into his eyes, a voice told me, 'You're going to marry this man.'" She hadn't even known his name.

"My mother—your grandmother—really had the gift," Mom said.

I nodded, although I wasn't sure where she was going with this. Grandma's letters to me, actually magic lessons, filled a green trunk under my bed. Even thinking of her shot happiness through my body.

"It was horrible," Mom said.

"What? What do you mean?"

"I don't mean that her gift was horrible, but my mother was always busy. Always in the garden messing with her herbs and plants. Neighbors were constantly at the back door, needing help with something—a cough, money trouble, husband with a wandering eye. She never had time for me."

It was strange to look at my mother and imagine her as a child. No wonder she'd become so responsible. No wonder she'd built a world of lists and willpower. No wonder she'd forced my grandmother to bind my magic. Until the tethers had snapped and I'd landed in Wilfred.

This was something that could happen to me, I realized. I was a truth teller who drew magic from books. It could consume me. It could even take my life, as it had my great-great-grandmother's, also a truth teller.

I rested my head on the side of my mother's shoulder. "Do you ever use your magic? Intentionally?"

I felt her head shake no. "Sometimes I get visions I can't help but see, but those are rare these days. No, I don't see the point. What will be, will be. I have enough to worry about without trying to bend fate."

"Back at the café, I thought you had a hit about Sam."

The pause before her reply put me on alert. "No, honey," she said. "You must have been mistaken."

As she spoke, her voice had hardened into the mom I knew from phone conversations with tips about my diet or career. Our tender exchange was over.

I stood. "Thanks, Mom, for the advice about Sam. I'll think it over."

CHAPTER FOUR

Then the letters began to arrive.

The day before, preparing to open for the week, I'd given Mom the grand tour of the library, hoping she'd experience some of the glory I'd felt when I'd first seen it. We walked through the library opening curtains and turning on lights. I showed her how the morning sun through the building's cupola splashed jewel tones on the atrium floor, soon to be washed out by electric lights when we opened for business. I pointed out the carved marble on my favorite fireplaces—each of the mansion's former bedrooms, now crammed with full bookshelves, had them—and the missing crystals on the chandeliers I loved regardless in the former parlor and dining room.

I showed her the card catalogs in their dovetailed walnut drawers and bragged how I'd installed a computer catalog system.

"Why keep the card catalogs, then?" Mom asked.

"Patrons insisted," I said.

She pointed to the heavy black telephone on the desk in Circulation. "Does that explain those ancient phones, too?"

"They work," I said. "Besides, at least they're not still party lines."

"You've got to be kidding."

"Not kidding. Once the mill shut down, the phone company practically wrote Wilfred off. We had one of the last party line systems in the state."

Over the worn Persian carpets we walked to the foyer, where I latched open the inner door and checked the book return box. Then we crossed the atrium to the conservatory. Lyndon had already propped up the heavy windows in the glass ceiling to let in cool morning air. He'd return midday to close them against the heat.

We ended our tour in the kitchen, where I started a pot of coffee. The kitchen library functioned as Wilfred's secondary town hall, after Darla's Café. Library regulars often bypassed the front door to enter through the kitchen, where they could sit for a cup of coffee before lounging with a newspaper in the mansion's former dining room, now Popular Fiction, or retreating to Natural History to peruse the wildlife of Tanzania before taking a cat nap on the couch. This was unorthodox behavior in a library, I knew, but as long as food and drink stayed in the kitchen—and, on occasion, the conservatory, where the knitting club met—I was satisfied.

Finally, I unlocked my office door and cranked open

its casement window to the swishing of the cotton-wood trees in the breeze along the Kirby River below. My office was just off the kitchen in the mansion's former pantry under the main staircase. Instead of rows of canned apricots and barrels of potatoes and onions, it now held a desk, a coat tree, bookshelves, and an armchair more often than not filled with a sleeping cat. The ceiling sloped because of the stairwell above, and if I stretched I could touch both walls with my hands, but I loved it.

Then, this morning, there it was on my desk: *Penning Poison: A History of Anonymous Letters*. Many evenings books settled themselves on my bedside table, often nonfiction having to do with dealing with patrons, and sometimes simply novels to relax or distract me. Finding a book in my locked office was another matter, and that the book was about poison-pen letters stopped me cold. I carefully set the book next to my laptop. I'd consider it later.

Just then, Roz, the assistant librarian, burst through the kitchen door. "The nerve!" she said.

"The nerve, what?"

"To accuse me of being a thief. As if." She waved a letter like a fan against her reddening neck. Roz was perpetually cranky, but, deep down, sweet hearted. Her dark hair and rosy cheeks, which might have graced an actress playing "country girl of a certain age," contradicted her dour approach to life. Someday her menopausal symptoms would lessen, but it was anyone's guess whether her mood swings would ever even out.

"Someone called you a thief?" I asked.

"Never mind. It's nonsense, anyway." Roz stormed through the kitchen on her way to the conservatory where she spent mornings writing romance novels as Eliza Chatterley Windsor.

The next incident came with the mail. Mom had wandered down to the café for a more hearty breakfast than the bowl of oatmeal I had on hand. Except for Roz and an apple-root-stock farmer browsing New Releases, I was alone in Circulation.

Derwin Garlington, the town's mail carrier, ambled through the library's front door and dropped a few periodicals and a bill on my desk. "None for you."

I glanced at the mail, then at him. "You mean, besides this stack."

"Right. I'm surprised, actually." Derwin's post-office-issue cap barely fit over his mop of brown hair.

"Surprised about what?"

"I figured you'd done something worth noting."

"Derwin, what are you talking about?"

He pushed up the bill of his cap. "The letters." His eyes narrowed. "Not that I know what's in them. It's a federal crime to read people's mail. I don't do that." He shook his head to emphasize the point. "But I can't help it if I'm there when someone opens a letter and has a freak-out."

With that, he hitched up his mail bag and left.

Confirmation came when Mom returned to the library. Nudging Rodney to the side, she dropped into the worn armchair near the circulation desk. The French doors to the garden between the library and Big House, where Sam lived, were open, and the scent of roses drifted in.

"I may never eat again," she said. "Those pancakes. So fluffy! With fresh raspberries. The kids we saw last night stopped me in the parking lot and offered to wash my car. I hated to tell them I'd walked."

Buffy and Thor. Typical.

"And remember the gentleman we saw at the Aerie when we arrived? The elegant one?"

"Emilio Landau, he said his name was."

Mom crossed her legs and leaned back. She was settling in for a gossip. "He's a picky eater. Had a Denver omelet."

"What's picky about that?"

"He only eats eggs in the morning, he told me. Never past noon." She smiled. "Isn't that adorable? His mustache is practically white, but he has one strand of black running through it."

I didn't like where this was going. "How long is he in town?"

Mom shook her head. "Don't know. He's staying at the Wallingford Guest House. You know the girl twirling batons last night on the patio? That's Ellie, the owners' daughter. I guess her parents won't send her to majorette camp, so she's trying to raise the money herself to go."

I shook my head. "I think people would chip in if it meant she'd leave us in peace. Last week she staged an impromptu show outside the library and we had to call the volunteer fire department to get her baton down from the oak tree."

"Emilio is looking to buy the Aerie. Make it his country retreat. I told him I could give him some pointers on the real estate contract."

That got my attention. "He knows you're married, right?"

She shrugged and looked away.

"Mom—"

She showed me her left hand, her ring finger still sporting its white gold wedding band. "We chatted. That's all. Don't get so upset."

I shot her my most disapproving look. When she didn't reply, I said, "I can't imagine the Duffys are selling the Aerie. Benjamin seemed so happy to be home."

Mom out and out ignored me. "Something strange was going on at the café. I sat at the counter, hoping to see what Darla puts in those grits. I swear, four or five people were looking at letters, scowling, and stuffing them back into their pockets. Darla even had one. I saw it under a pile of menus next to the milkshake machine. Nobody said anything, but it didn't take a psychic to know something was off."

Of course, Mom *was* a psychic. Noting her artful turn of conversation, I made a note to return to the Emilio Landau discussion later. "What were the letters about?"

She held up both palms. "Don't know. It's none of my business."

"Oh, Mom. Really? Didn't you catch a drift at all?"

She looked at a paisley woven into the carpet. "I don't do that, Josie. I have better uses for my energy."

The book giving a history of anonymous letters;

Roz accused of being a thief; Derwin's cryptic comments; Mom's observations. Someone was writing poison-pen letters. How and why—and what would come of it—remained to be seen.

When I arrived at Sam's that evening—a short stroll across the lawn separating the library from Big House—he was filleting a salmon. I loved watching him work in the kitchen. He'd rolled up his sleeves, and those sensitive fingers wielded the knife like a maestro. A pile of herbs, chopped on a wooden cutting board, sat to the side. The kitchen smelled of basil and roses. How did I get so lucky?

The kitchen door was propped open to let in the summer evening breeze off the river. I fastened the baby gate behind me, but not before Rodney squeezed in. Nicky, getting to be a pro at walking, squealed at Rodney, repeating, "Baht, baht," his word for "cat." Fitting, since Rodney's sleek black fur gave him a bat-like air.

"I hope your mom likes fish," Sam said.

"She's not coming tonight," I said. "Didn't you get my text?"

Sam wiped his hands. "No. No text."

I glanced at my phone. "That's odd. My phone says it was sent."

Sam returned to the fillet. "I might have missed it."

I wasn't so sure. Since spring, I'd had the feeling of a veil of trouble wafting over me. Sometimes I barely noticed it—it was simply a fleeting intuition that something wasn't right. Other days, signs arose everywhere: the crows that followed me, flitting from branch to branch; fruit that deadened in the bowl overnight; hiccups in my communications with the books; and now these glitches in communication with Sam.

I couldn't talk to Sam about it. Once he knew I was a witch, I could bring it up. That was still a hurdle to overcome.

"I've been busy lately. We have a big case right now—one of my old FBI colleagues is even involved."

"What's the case about?"

"Top secret," he said.

We often discussed Sam's work, and he'd benefitted from my insight more than once. It irked me that he wouldn't say more. "Just a hint? If the FBI is involved, it's not local."

Sam pulled a skillet from a cupboard. "No, not local. I can tell you that much. It's not my investigation, though, so I have to keep mum." He turned to me and placed a hand on my arm. "You understand, don't you?"

I reluctantly nodded.

"Good." He returned to the stove. "What's your mother up to tonight? Staying in with—oh, I don't know—a book?"

I smiled, thinking of the thousands of library books silently calling to my mother. Then I frowned. "Mom wants a divorce."

Sam turned, knife in hand. "Oh, Josie."

"She told me yesterday. She's out with Emilio Landau tonight. They're going for a walk." I perched at the edge of the table. "I don't know if you can call it a date, but I don't like it."

"Emilio Landau, huh?" He thoughtfully set down the knife. "Maybe they'll take the trail that circles by the retreat center. The yodeling workshop should squelch any thoughts of romance."

"I doubt Dad has any idea of what's going on. My mother could slide divorce papers right under his nose, and unless they were written in medieval French, he wouldn't even notice. I called my sister Toni and asked her to check in with him." Nicky pulled at my pant leg. I hoisted him to a hip and kissed his chubby cheek. "I halfway wonder if he even knows she's not home."

"If I ever do anything like that, you'll tell me, right? Even if it's decades from now?" Sam's voice had softened.

Decades from now. He imagined being with me that long. I let Nicky down and put my arms around Sam. How could my mother leave my father if she'd ever felt for him a fraction of what I felt for Sam?

Over Sam's shoulder, I caught a glimpse of an envelope sticking out from under the day's mail. The letter murmured in low, threatening tones. I pulled back. "Sam, what's that letter?"

"It's the craziest thing. Look at it."

The envelope was a thick cream vellum addressed to Sam in block letters. No return address. I took it to the table and pulled out a chair. The letter inside was on plain printer paper, but even before unfolding it, I could tell it was no ordinary note. I flattened it on the tabletop. Its message was cut from a magazine—single letters here, whole words there—and glued to the paper. *Your family robbed its workers. You will pay*, it said. That was all.

I refolded the letter. "What's this about?"

"Some crank. By now it's common knowledge that my parents short-shrifted the mill workers when they left town, but that was thirty years ago."

Sam—Sam Wilfred—was descended from Thurston Wilfred, who'd built the timber mill that had founded the town. In the early nineteen-nineties, Sam's parents had abruptly closed the mill and fled, leaving hundreds of workers without paychecks. To make amends, Sam had donated the land the mill once stood on to Wilfred, and the retreat center had been built near the old millpond. As far as I knew, Wilfredians considered the debt settled.

"Isn't there a law about these kinds of letters?" I asked.

"The one I received doesn't contain a threat—at least, not a specific threat. Someone might be able to press charges, saying the letters were harassment, but it would be a weak case."

That didn't make it right. "Word on the street is that you're not the only person who's received one."

"Have you?" Sam asked.

"No. Not yet at least." The suspicion, the fear that the letters might engender. Maybe Sam could laugh off his letter, but it didn't mean everyone would. "I really don't like that last line."

"'You will pay,'" Sam repeated. "Yes, that's the part that gets me." Salmon now in the oven, he took the chair next to mine. "As I said, it's probably some crank. Have you seen the other letters?"

"No. I think Roz got one, and Derwin said he'd delivered a few others."

Nicky waddled over, raising his arms to his father. Sam lifted him into his lap and picked up a fresh bib from the table.

"I'm sure it's nothing," Sam said. "It will blow over. Wilfred is a strong town that way."

CHAPTER FIVE

When a storm is brewing, the air thickens and electrifies with static. My curly hair acts as a barometer, frizzing a notice of rain more reliably than any weather app. The sky bruises gray-brown, and the wind picks up. You know a storm is on its way, but you don't know how violently the rain will pelt and lightning slash.

That was the feeling I had now. It wasn't about the weather—that remained a steady, cloudless heat. It was a storm of circumstances I felt building around me. Something was going to happen. Something big. But what?

As often occurred in times like these, I felt the pull of my grandmother's magic lessons. Somehow knowing I would come into my magic after she died, my grandmother had written a series of letters on magic and life, each sealed in an envelope and stored with her grimoire in a green trunk. That trunk was under my bed now.

Before I could choose a lesson, I made sure my mother was comfortably installed in the tower room. She'd come home distracted and slightly dreamy after her walk with Emilio Landau, which had turned into dinner, too.

"Nothing happened, honey," she'd assured me.

"It better not have," I'd growled. I still hadn't heard back from Toni about Dad.

"We talked real estate. That's all. Listened to a few yodelers. Emilio has plans for the Aerie. Structural things first—you know, new windows, solid roof."

I drew back my head. "Do you know for sure they're selling?" Remembering Benjamin's lit-up expression at being home and the warming sight of the reunited brothers making music on the deck, I would have put money on their staying put.

"Emilio can be very convincing. I'm sure he'll find a way to have what he wants."

I didn't like the sound of this and drilled my stare into her. "Did you call Dad tonight?"

"It's three hours later there, Josie. I didn't want to wake him up. I'll call in the morning."

I left Mom reaching for a mystery novel on the bed-side table. Rodney jumped off her bed and followed me back to my bedroom. I opened my apartment windows for the breeze and lit a candle. The letters under my bed almost sang to me—a choir of love and warning. Rodney's purr geared up a notch.

I opened the trunk and let my hand glide through the envelopes until one warmed and pulled itself into my grasp. This was it—this was tonight's lesson.

"Come on, Rodney." I didn't have to ask him twice.

He leapt to the bed and settled in my lap as I ripped open the sealed letter, releasing the scent of my grandmother's kitchen: lavender, rosemary, and something spicy on the stove. Grandma's voice, sweet and loving, read to me.

> *Dear Josie,*
> *Tonight I want to tell you about secrets—about their purpose, their pitfalls, and how to respect them.*
> *As I write, I see you in a tall wooden bed with Victorian carving. Could that be true?*

I glanced up at my ornate walnut headboard, likely Old Man Thurston's bed hauled up from the master bedroom when it became Natural History. My grandmother hadn't been known for the gift of foresight—that was my mother's gift—but magic worked mysteriously, and occasionally reflections of other gifts flashed through a witch's abilities.

> *Today, many people disdain secrets by saying things like, "I'm an open book" or "honesty is the best policy." Certainly, dishonesty is never a good policy, and I know how you love books, open or not. However, secrets have their place, and many secrets are best kept that way.*
> *You are bound to keep secrets that are not yours—as long as no one is hurt by keeping them. Mrs. Rombauer never told anyone her neighbor was regularly abused by her husband.*

"Not my business," she said. "She told me not to say anything." Whether it was fastidiousness, lack of courage, or simple indifference that persuaded Mrs. Rombauer to keep this secret, it led to her neighbor's broken ribs.

Other secrets may only cause harm if they're revealed. For instance, your mother tints her hair. What would be the good of spreading that fact around?

Then there are secrets that should not be kept, not because, as in the case of Mrs. Rombauer, keeping them will hurt someone else, but because not revealing them hurts you. They need to be shared, but sharing them comes with a cost. Perhaps this is why you have come to this lesson today. I urge you to examine not what sharing the secret will cost you, but the true cost of keeping it.

Is this secret about your magic? If so, I certainly understand why you'd hesitate to reveal it. Letting others know you're a witch could put you at risk. For generations, women in our family have hidden our magic. It's what has permitted us to survive. Our power threatens too many people to make us safe. However, if you have found someone to spend your life with, you must consider telling him you're a witch. Yes, you risk losing him. Magic is something many people can't accept. But if you don't tell him, you will have kept from him a fundamental part of who you are. He can never truly know you.

I set the letter in my lap a moment, and Rodney rested a black velvet paw on it. Grandma had hit upon the truth. I needed to tell Sam about my magic. Yet I dreaded it. Loving him was the best thing that had ever happened to me, and I didn't want to lose that. I couldn't simply turn off my magic and become a regular citizen and keep Sam that way, either. My life was not an episode of *Bewitched*. Without magic, I was another person, and I couldn't go back. Before I came into my magic, it was as if I'd seen the world through a scrim. Magic tightened my focus, and now the sky was bluer, the smell of the cottonwoods sweeter, and the tug of a smile—Sam's smile—on my heart was keener. I couldn't give that up.

> *Maybe that's not it. Maybe this has to do with other people's secrets, secrets that are or will come into play in your life.*
>
> *You can know these secrets, Josie, if you want. Your magic will reveal them to you, if you listen closely. The books will tell you, explicitly or less so, the secrets you seek to reveal if you ask them. What I ask you is, do you really want to know? And what is the cost associated with using your magic to delve into the lives of others?*
>
> *I love you so much, honey. That love is another kind of magic that is always with you. Remember that.*

I kissed the letter and returned it to its envelope. My world was neck-deep in secrets these days. Mom's intent to divorce Dad, the accusations in the anonymous letters, and, of course, my hidden magic.

Which secrets did this lesson concern? Maybe all of them. I'd soon know.

CHAPTER SIX

At the library the next morning, no one spoke about the letters, but they were always present, buzzing in people's minds and showing in their rattled responses and suspicious glances. Only one person had his letter with him, one of the Stimson brothers. I heard the letter's accusing voice from where it was folded in his back pocket. *"You told your cousin not to marry the Fastvall girl, not because she was loose, as you claimed, but because you wanted her for yourself. You will pay."*

Even Derwin, the mail carrier, looked out of sorts. Yesterday, he'd seemed curious about the letters—even prurient. Today he kept his head down when he made his rounds. He dropped a bundle of mail on the circulation desk and was out the door in record time.

I was sorting through the stack when Patty cleared her throat. I looked up to find her, hands clasped at chest height, at my side. "Can I help you find anything?" I asked.

The books were generally quick with suggestions and sent their titles to me in rapid fire. However, patrons didn't always want to cop to what they truly wanted—or needed—to read. I'd learned the hard way not to suggest, unless asked, articles on bunion removal or reinvigorating a stale marriage. Patty, Darla's sister and owner of the This-N-That across the street from the café, was generally a curious, upbeat person. Until she'd hit upon the idea of converting her shop into an antiques mall, she'd combed the region to fill the shelves with whatever her latest enthusiasm was, from bells and scissors to candles and birdcages. So I was surprised when the titles that whispered to me through the ether were self-help books on managing depression.

Patty looked at the carpet, at the fireplace mantel behind me, and out the French doors. "I don't know."

"You're in a library, Patty. Could it be you're looking for something to read? Or maybe information?" When she didn't respond, I added, "What's wrong?"

"Nothing," came her hasty reply. "How's your mother?"

"Fine." She was out with Emilio Landau. I didn't want to talk about it. "A new book came in on home weight-lifting routines for women." Besides shopping to fill the shelves at the This-N-That, exercise and diet obsessed Patty—at least, learning about it and amassing athletic wear did. However, I'd never actually seen her so much as perform a single jumping jack, and her special "smoothies" were more likely to contain strawberry ice cream than protein powder.

"No, thank you."

"There have been a lot of poison-pen letters going

around, I hear," I prompted. "I don't suppose you got one?" As I spoke, the books whispered titles to me, all with the theme of mending family relationships. What was up?

"I don't know anything about that," she said.

Patty was down about something, but she wouldn't tell me about it. That much was clear. Maybe I could help, anyway. I picked up a volume from the cart of books to reshelve. "Montgomery just finished a collection of stories by P. G. Wodehouse." Montgomery was Darla's husband, an import from her beloved South. "He said they really cheered him up. Maybe you'd like to read them?"

"All right," she said finally. "I guess that will do."

Patty left with the book, and I returned to the mail. There it was, at the bottom of the pile: a letter for me with no return address. I stared at it for a heartbeat, then two. Through the thick white envelope, I felt its contents growl. This was bad. I squeezed my fingers into fists and released them and fumbled for the letter opener.

Unlike the other letters, mine was written by hand—no glued-on words cut from magazines. Its message was simple, in black ink: *I know your secret.* That was all.

I stood, the letter dangling from my fingers. Who wrote this? The secret it mentioned—did someone know I was a witch? My breath came quickly.

Rodney hopped to the desk and, hackles raised, backed away from the letter. He hissed and jumped to the floor.

I grabbed my phone. I needed to tell Sam—or did I? No. First I needed to think through how to respond. Maybe the letter was simply someone fishing for a reaction, trying to get me upset. After all, unlike Sam's and Roz's letters, no "secret" in particular had been mentioned.

As I was returning my phone to my purse, Patty burst back into Circulation. She put a hand on the door frame and another on her chest as she gasped. "It's . . . it's . . ."

"Are you okay, Patty?"

Catching her breath, she nodded. "It's Benjamin Duffy."

Benjamin. Reverend Duffy's son, newly returned from New York. "What about him?"

"He's dead."

CHAPTER SEVEN

"Benjamin Duffy is what?" I led Patty to a chair. "What happened?"

Patty sank into the cushions and let out a long breath, pressing her palm to her chest. "He fell. Off the deck of the Aerie. I was upstairs and saw the volunteer fire truck go by."

I knew how these things worked. She would have telephoned Margie at dispatch and extracted the whole story.

"Adam and Lucy found him," Patty added. "Just awful."

I still couldn't believe it. Benjamin Duffy? Dead? "That railing didn't look very sturdy." Yet, he'd known better. It was Benjamin who'd warned Mom not to lean on it. I glanced at the poison-pen letter still in my hand and slipped it out of sight under my desk blotter. "It couldn't have been on purpose, could it?"

"You mean, could he have jumped?" She leaned back, considering this angle. "Maybe he got one of the letters. Didn't want his wife to know." She tapped a finger against her jaw then shook her head. "Nope. Don't see it. First, he's been home only, what, a month? Not long enough to document wrongdoings. Besides, I hear he had a troubled past." She gave me a meaningful look. How she got that information, I wasn't sure. "Why would something in a letter distress him enough to take his own life?"

"When I saw him at his father's estate sale, he seemed happy to be home," I said.

A few patrons had edged near us. One pretended to scan the shelf of DVDs, and the other, mouth agape, listened openly.

Patty nodded. "Benjamin and Adam were such good kids, even as teens. They played music together at the church. I swear half of Wilfred drove up to Marlin Hill just to hear their bluegrass take on 'The Old Rugged Cross.' It wasn't to hear Reverend Duffy's sermons. That's for sure."

"What do you mean?" I glanced at the room's other patrons. They seemed to be multiplying.

Patty summoned a "get closer, let's talk" look. "You must have gotten a feel for the old reverend at his estate sale."

I remembered his office's heaviness, the doom-chanting energy of the crated books, the roped-off entrance to his wife's bedroom. "Not exactly cheerful, was he?"

That was all the encouragement Patty needed. "The reverend wasn't like a normal pastor, spreading upbeat homilies and happy to receive homemade casseroles. I always had the feeling he judged me, even when I was doing something as innocent as washing the This-N-That's windows. He didn't dress normally, either."

"What do you mean?"

"Dressed like an old-time pastor," one of the nearby patrons said, her charade of not listening having ended. She clasped a best-selling fantasy novel. "Wore dark clothes, dark shoes."

"Like a character in a Dickens novel," added another patron, this one in work clothes that might have also been at home in Dickens, perhaps in a workhouse scene in *Oliver Twist*.

The first patron pulled up a chair. The second took her lead, and a few other patrons leaned against bookshelves, eliciting coos from the books behind them.

"What I don't get is what happened with the wife," a mom said. She balanced one child on her hip. Twin girls on the floor next to her quietly turned the pages of a picture book whispering circus music.

"The wife." Patty warmed to her audience. "That was quite a story."

She paused long enough that the patron with the Dickens comparison said, "Enough of this drama, Patty. Get on with it."

"We all loved Candy," she said. At my look of surprise—shouldn't a pastor's wife be named something less like an exotic dancer?—Patty added, "Yes, Candy. Short for Candace. Such a sweet woman. And that laugh!"

"Like a drunken donkey," the fantasy reader said. "Absolutely contagious."

"How did she die?" I asked.

"Accident," Patty said. "Tripped and fell. Physical exercise, including maintaining balance, is vital for women. That's why I stay on top of it."

We all resisted replying to that one.

"The boys were only in their teens. Such a shame," Mrs. Garlington added from the doorway. She was here to prepare for an organ lesson upstairs just after the library closed for the day. Otherwise people would never be able to concentrate with warbly scales and strains of "Release Me" reverberating through the atrium. "A few years later, Benjamin left."

"Reverend Duffy changed when Candy died. Slowly dropped off pastoring and became a shut-in. I always wondered if he blamed himself for her death." Patty let out a sigh. "I guess we'll never know."

"Sad," one patron said.

"Very sad," added another.

We sat in silence for a moment, pondering this turn of events.

Now that Patty had regained her breath, she popped up, eyes bright. "Got to run. There might be new intelligence at the café."

I slipped my letter from under the blotter into my pocket and, lost in thought, returned to the circulation desk.

She Shall Have Murder, a book whispered from the shelves.

That evening I closed the library in record time, shutting off lights and drawing curtains against the still-light early evening. The old mansion was practically empty, anyway, except for a farmworker studying English in the far reaches of Arts and Language. I put on my cheerful librarian voice and invited him back the next day.

Once the word of Benjamin's death dropped, Wilfredians had flooded to the café, on the alert for developments. Meanwhile, the library's stacks were alive with books murmuring titles. *The Dreadful Hollow*, *Poison in the Pen*, *The Crimson Madness of Little Doom*, *Fear Stalks the Village*. Aside from a reference to Dorothy L. Sayers's *Gaudy Night*, I didn't know these novels, but I was sure they shared the theme of poison-pen letters. My own letter burned in my pocket.

After I clicked off the last lamp, I took the stairs two at a time to my apartment to find Mom on the phone. She sat in the armchair by the fireplace with Rodney flicking his tale from his perch on the headrest.

"Oh, here comes Josie. I'll talk to you later." Mom glanced at me, then toward the window and laughed. "All right, goodbye."

"Dad?" I said hopefully.

She set her phone face down on the side table. "No. Don't give me that look, Joséphine."

It had been Emilio Landau—slippery as his emblematic eel—on the phone. Had to be. I tamped down my irritation and handed my letter to my mother. First things first. "This came in the mail today."

Mom reached for the envelope, her expression rigid with concern even before she'd read it. My heart dropped. Given Mom's gift of sight, her anxiety couldn't be good. I watched her face as she read it and saw her features firm into an even, impassive look, a reaction I'd seen her take many times over the decades. She would give nothing away.

I expelled a long breath. "What do you think?"

She refolded the letter and returned it to its envelope. "You have to tell Sam."

"About the letter?" I knew what Mom had meant, but I didn't want to acknowledge it.

"That you're a witch. This note"—she waved the envelope—"might be nothing more than a fishing expedition. On the other hand, someone might know about you." She leaned forward, and Rodney's tail brushed her cheek. "Does anyone have the slightest hint about your magic? Have you done anything—carried out a spell, moved objects without touching them—that someone might have seen?"

I dropped to the couch. Rodney leapt from the chair to the cushion next to me in one fluid motion, and I absently stroked the silky fur between his ears. "I'm pretty cautious, but it's possible."

Maybe even probable. Library patrons noted my uncanny ability to suggest the books they needed to read—even if they hadn't known it. After closing hours, I sometimes used magic to aid cleanup. I could gather the books' energy and thrust open my arms to send books flying back to their shelves. But I always made sure the curtains were drawn first—or did I? Magic was so exhilarating that I might have been tempted once or twice to call a book to my hand or make an unrelated reading suggestion when the library was open. But I'd been careful. Or had I?

Mom settled back into the armchair. "You're serious about Sam, right?"

I nodded vigorously. "Of course."

"Then he needs to know you're a witch. You've got to tell him sometime. You don't want him to find out from someone else, do you?"

I glanced at the letter. It looked deceptively innocent—bland, almost. Strangely, I'd gotten no hit from it. It was as if all its energy had been wiped clean. "You're right. I do need to tell him." Yet, the risk. First, would he even believe me? *Honey, I'm a witch.* I didn't see that going well. Sam worked with evidence. Magic wouldn't be part of his lexicon. He would laugh. He would think I'd lost my mind.

Then, say he did eventually believe me. Would he want to be partnered with a freak of nature?

I knew who could tell me. "Mom? Do you—?"

"No. I will not be part of this."

"I'm not asking you to intervene. I just want to know how he'll respond. You can use my emotion for a read. Can't you give me a hint?" I studied her face.

Mom retreated behind an unreadable mask. "You know I don't do that." She let her arms slacken against the chair. "This isn't a matter of life and death, honey. The worst that can happen is he'll break your heart." Her voice softened. "You'll survive that. If it happens at all. You need to say something to him, though."

Words rushed to my lips. I could suggest I wait just a bit longer, until cool weather returned or life was more stable. But these were excuses.

Mom was right. Every day with Sam was a day of

lying by omission. I did need to tell him, and there would never be a perfect time. I didn't want him to learn from a stranger—especially one whose motives were unclear. Besides, Mom was here to comfort me. No one could tell me I was too old to cry on her shoulder.

"All right," I said. "Tomorrow night, when he gets home from work. I'll tell him then." I eyed my mother. "I suppose you can find something to keep yourself busy?"

Emilio Landau's name floated between us in the ether. She nodded.

As Mom drew a breath to reply, Rodney launched from the sofa toward the open window. A chill deeper than a January midnight seeped over me. Rodney growled. A crow cawed and spread its wings wide to fly away.

CHAPTER EIGHT

I shook off the feeling of foreboding and stood. "Let's get out of the house. Come on. You've been here two full days and haven't even had a proper tour of town." Maybe I'd get more out of Mom about her plans if we were moving. Besides, someone might have new information about the anonymous letters.

"Emilio and I walked all through Wilfred yesterday."

"He's not a local. I'll introduce you around." Summer days were long this time of year, and it wasn't even dinnertime. Mom and I made our way down the stairs to the side exit.

"I used to go for walks with your father," Mom said. "It was nice."

"Why did you stop?" I locked the library behind us. Rodney burst out the cat door and trotted ahead.

"Oh, you know. You girls came along, and suddenly my days were filled with making lunches and taking you all to band practice and science club."

"And now?" I asked.

Mom and I looked at each other. Even Rodney, a few yards ahead, turned to stare. Mom's excuses no longer applied. If she wanted to, she could walk weekly marathons with Dad through the neighborhood.

"Emilio says walking is key to mental and physical health. He says he can't wait to take daily strolls through Marlin Hill."

Emilio says. I was ready to jump on that, but the reminder about the Aerie nudged my thoughts to a different track. "It's hardly a good time to talk real estate. Both Lucy and Adam will be grieving."

"Maybe they'll be in a better mind to sell now."

"That sounds predatory to me," I said.

"You don't know their situation, Josie. They might welcome the opportunity to move on."

We arrived at the stone bridge crossing the Kirby River. It was one of my favorite vantage points on Wilfred. Now, at the height of summer, the blue-green river sleepwalked its way beneath a moving curtain of cottonwoods. Behind us, the library's tower rose above oaks and conifers with the peak of Big House's roof nearby. Below us, the town spread into the valley with the retreat center at its far left, then, closer, the Magnolia Rolling Estates and the café. The few square blocks of downtown Wilfred, such as it was, straddled the quiet old highway.

"There's Darla's Café, where we had dinner last night," I told Mom.

"The parking lot is nearly full, and it's not even five o'clock."

"It's the only place in town to hang out. Except the

library," I said. "There, on the other side of the road is the This-N-That—Darla's sister Patty owns it. Two storefronts down used to be the Empress, an old movie theater, but it's been closed for years." I pointed a few blocks east. "That's the church and churchyard. There's a Grange hall at the edge of town. Basically, that's it. That's Wilfred."

"Don't forget the Wallingford Guest House," Mom said. "There it is."

"I see. They've really fixed it up." In the house's backyard, the glint of batons twirling caught my eye.

"Emilio says Wilfred isn't bad for such a small town."

"Could we not talk about Emilio Landau for a minute?" I said.

"I don't know what you're getting so upset about. It's not like anything improper is going on."

I huffed and looked at her. Something about being with Mom yanked me back to my teens. "Come on. I'll take you to the This-N-That to meet a few people. Maybe Babe Hamilton will be in. I think you'll like her."

When we opened the This-N-That's front door, instead of a chime, the united voices of Buffy and Thor greeted us.

"Hello," Buffy said from her seat on the counter. Today she wore a lime lamé tank top with a princess's head on it, shorts, and silver high-heeled sandals meant for a full-grown woman. If I knew Patty, the sandals would go the moment she clapped eyes on them.

"Welcome," Thor said at the same time. Due to the heat, Thor sported a cropped version of his usual cape.

A pink line worn into his temple showed he'd removed his ornamental eyepatch only minutes earlier.

"For a small consideration," Buffy said, "we'd be happy to show you the best of what Grandma's This-N-That has to offer."

"The most interesting items and best deals," Thor added.

"No thanks," I told them. "We're looking for Babe. I want my mom to meet her."

"She just left," Buffy said. "But I could find her. For a—"

"Small consideration," I finished. Where had she learned that term? "That's okay. I'll just show Mom around."

"Suit yourself," Thor said, rubbing his temple where the eyepatch's elastic band had worried at his skin. "We'll stay here and count our bank." He pulled a wad of one-dollar bills from the back pocket of his shorts.

"Where did you get all that?" Buffy and Thor were constantly on the prowl for money, but they weren't usually so successful.

"Ten big ones," Thor said.

"Thor, don't tell. Remember? We promised," Buffy said.

"It was a mysterious task. Mysterious and nutritive."

"You mean 'lucrative,' Thor. Never mind," I said.

Mom was already in Babe's booth at the front of the store. She ran a hand over a linen sheet. "This is where you bought your bedding, isn't it?"

"Yes. Isn't this great?" I lifted a panel from a stack of midcentury bark-cloth curtains splattered with hibiscus flowers. Ever since my magic had awakened, my senses had, too. I was wild for pattern and texture now and found myself at Babe's booth practically weekly looking for vintage linen dishtowels and delicate cotton handkerchiefs. I loved the handwork—fine embroidery and monograms—and each item felt full of story. Plus, Babe was always open for a chat. She was quickly becoming a friend and confidante.

Mom yanked back her palm and kept her hand close to her body. "Sure. Great."

"What?" Something had disturbed my mother. We couldn't talk openly about any psychic hit she may have had from the sheet—not with Buffy and Thor so near—but Mom had definitely felt some sort of flash. I'd ask her later, which didn't guarantee she'd respond.

"Hi, Josie." Lalena stood in the entrance to Babe's booth. Ian was behind her in his wheelchair with Lalena's terrier mutt, Sailor, in his lap. The stacks of sheets and colorful curtains made a fitting frame for the old French chemise Lalena wore. "Did you hear about Benjamin Duffy?"

"I did," I said. "I feel awful. He seemed so happy to be back. Plus, poor Adam. First his father, then this."

She nodded and rested a hand on Ian's shoulder. "They say there was an empty whiskey bottle on the deck." Something murmured from Lalena's vicinity. I glanced behind her. The voice—melancholic, insistent—didn't come from a person. No one else was in the store. A book wanted to tell me something.

"He'd had too much to drink and fell?"

"That's what Adam thinks. The sad part is that Benjamin had been sober for over a year."

His father's death, the move, being reunited with

family—all of this might have tipped him into a relapse. A shame. The nearby voice whispered, "incompetence."

I affected a blasé tone. "Say, Lalena. You didn't happen to get one of the letters that are going around? Or maybe you, Ian?"

Ian rolled back a few inches. "Not me."

"I did." Lalena pulled the now all-too-familiar envelope from her carpet bag. "Look. It accuses my family of letting certain people, especially attractive ladies, get off traffic tickets at the speed trap." Sam's installment in Wilfred had interrupted three generations of sheriffs, all related to Lalena. For decades, Wilfredians had been used to greeting the sheriff, no matter who it was, with "Hello, Sheriff Dolby."

Lalena's letter was, like the others, written in words and letters cut from a magazine and pasted in place. So far, mine was the only letter in pen. As with the others, her letter concluded with "you will pay."

"So strange," I said. "Who's writing these things?"

"I don't know," Lalena replied. "But it's messing with people. I went to get my mail, and Mrs. Blanche watched me, blatantly, the whole time like she was afraid I'd steal hers. At the café, Cheryl shot daggers at me just for saying hello to her husband. Even Patty and Darla won't talk to each other."

That explained Patty's mood earlier today. "That's terrible."

"Everyone's suspicious. And angry."

"I've got to get back to my stall to unpack a couple of boxes from the reverend's estate," Ian said.

Buffy and Thor loitered behind him, likely ready to

suggest a task they could carry out for a "small consideration."

I followed Ian to his stall to glance at his shelves. The smell of mildew rose from the crates from the estate sale, but no particular messages came to me. Whatever it was the book had wanted to say was moot now. "We should be moving on, too," I said.

Outside the shop, a crow watched from his perch on a fence post, its feathers shimmering with heat. This was too much. "What do you want?" I asked it.

Behind me, my mother said, "Josie?"

"The crows. They've been following me for months."

"Lower your voice." Mom nodded toward the café across the street, where diners lounged on the patio. "It's just a bird."

The crow flew up to perch on the gutter.

"It's more than that," I said. "Something strange is going on. It's not just the crows, either. Creepy things have been happening." Benjamin's tragic accident, the letters, the crows, the foreboding energy. Were they related? What was going on?

The sun was lowering, but the evening was still warm. Mom lifted her hair from her neck. "Let's go home, and you can tell me all about it."

CHAPTER NINE

At last, night was falling, and cooler air came with it. While Mom made herbal tea—a blend of lavender and chamomile I kept for evenings like this—I circled my apartment, opening windows for the relief of a cross breeze. When I returned to the living room, lit candles glowed from the fireplace mantel, bookcase, and coffee table.

"Candles? On a summer night?" I asked Mom.

"Your grandmother always said they helped focus her energy. You're going to tell me something important, and I figured they couldn't hurt." She fluffed the pillow on the armchair and sat. "Besides, the beeswax smells nice."

Maybe Mom was opening up to her magic after all. I poured tea for us. "I don't know who else to tell about it. We're the only witches I know. And I'm not sure where to begin."

"At the beginning, of course."

I sat back. "It started in early spring." The rain, the wet trees, and the cold. "I began to notice crows."

"Crows," Mom said.

"I know, I know. Cliché, right? Crows are everywhere. Why should seeing a few crows be a big deal?" I edged forward. "But I swear they were watching me. Plus, they appeared all the time, even at night when they should have been nesting."

"How did you feel?"

"They disturbed me. Something was off-kilter."

"That's not all," Mom said with certainty.

"Right. At first I was willing to dismiss the crows as a fluke. What did I know about the bird world?" However, I had discussed the crows with Ruth Littlewood, Wilfred's resident bird expert, and she'd told me what I'd seen was impossible. "Then other things happened. First, they were small, then they seemed to gather strength." Strangely, my tongue thickened. I had trouble making words. "Then . . ." The evening light seemed to dim all at once. I had to focus simply to breathe.

"Then what?"

"Like . . . like . . ." The sentences wouldn't come. Each time I opened my mouth, it was as if my tongue had turned to sludge. I forced my lungs to fill.

Mom stood. "Josie?"

"What?" Even that word was difficult to form. My eyes closed.

"Something is happening here. Cast a circle."

My eyes flew open and my gaze shot to Mom in surprise. Grandma's letters had taught me about casting circles to protect against bad energy, but I hadn't had to practice it here, where the books cradled me in their protective aura.

"My mother used to do this when neighbors talked about her." Mom yanked me to my feet. "Something is interfering with us. Cast a circle."

"Okay." Mom steadied me, and after a few breaths I could move, although slowly. "I'm ready."

Rodney appeared from nowhere, as he often did when I corralled my magic. With hard effort, I raised my arms to draw from the energy that countless authors and readers had put into the library's books. Slowly, my head began to clear. Mom seemed to feel it, too. She looked more alert, more alive.

I closed my eyes and remembered my grandmother's instructions. I walked due north and turned to face the living room as the star-shaped birthmark on my shoulder burned with power. "I draw upon the books to surround me and my mother, to protect us from any energy that does not contribute to our greater good."

At once, a thick band of story layered behind me. I felt caravans, teenagers coming of age, wizened kings, battle-scared generals, and sniping would-be lovers weave into a protective barrier stronger than cast-iron mesh. Wielding this energy behind me like a powerful cape, I circled the room, depositing it behind, around, below, and above us. At last I returned to the couch.

An impenetrable yet invisible shield now protected us. The shield hummed a background noise of story so interwoven that it became static. A featherlight peace had settled inside the circle. Whatever it was that had sought to silence me had itself been silenced.

"That's better." Mom's concern morphed into admiration. "Your abilities are amazing."

"I'm amazed, myself," I said. "It really works. What do you think was here with us?"

"I don't know, honey. I wonder if my being here antagonized it?"

I considered this. "Maybe. But what does it want?"

Mom shook her head. "I don't know, but it's gone. Now, tell me more."

I took a few breaths to recenter myself, then told Mom about some of the bizarre happenings, including the incident with the mirror and the unpredictable miscommunications with Sam. I squeezed my eyes shut and opened them again. "Most of the time, it's little things. But once, last spring . . ."

"Last spring, what?"

I shivered, remembering. "Just down from the This-N-That is the Empress, a boarded-up movie theater. It's been closed for almost fifty years. I pointed it out to you tonight." When she nodded, I continued. "I was inside, alone, and the air froze. I could see my breath. Then images appeared on the screen." My throat tightened. "I'm pretty sure one of them was Grandma. From before I was born. She said, 'Be gone.' Then the images vanished."

"A banishment spell," Mom said.

"It's as if a force rolls in to block my energy. That was the strongest show of it yet. Then, tonight . . ."

"Tell me more." Mom's voice was soothing. She stroked Rodney, who purred like a lawnmower within our protective circle.

"Sometimes when I'm marshaling my magic, even

to do something that comes easily, like summoning book titles, I can't break through. Some other energy seems to descend and voids my magic."

Mom lifted the teacup and examined its lavender-tinted contents. She returned the cup to its saucer. "When does this happen?"

"I can't predict it." The only witches I knew were in our family. With my mother here, I dared to ask the question I hadn't wanted to ponder sooner. "Could another witch be messing with me?"

Mom bit her lip and released it. "It's possible. Assume it's true. Why would someone want to interfere with your magic? Who and why now? What would they hope to gain?"

"I don't know. How would someone know I was a witch, anyway?"

Mom rested back in her chair. "I don't have answers." She tapped the chair's arms. "When you noticed the crows, was anyone new in town?"

I thought back to March. Wilfred was growing slowly, thanks to the retreat center, and we did have a few new residents. "The Wallingfords—you know, the people with the new guesthouse. The retreat center hired staff, but none of them live in town. Babe Hamilton and Ian Penclosa at the This-N-That. Maybe others I can't think of right now."

Of these names, Ian's stood out. The paranormal fascinated him, and he was notoriously cagey about his background. Yet he was almost too obvious. A devious witch would choose better cover.

"Tell me about our family," I said.

Mom's thoughts were clearly far away—on Dad?

On my predicament?—and it took her a moment to redirect her attention. "What do you want to know?"

"About the witch part." I edged closer. "All I know is that magic comes through the women in our family, and that we go back to Scotland. That and that every few generations a super-witch is born." Like me. And my grandmother. "I know each of us has her own source of power and her own sphere of action." I drew my magic from books, and I was a truth teller compelled to seek justice. Then I realized something. "Your gift is foresight, but I don't think I've ever known how you use it, what your sphere is."

"The truth is . . ." Mom's hands fell to her sides.

"Yes?"

"The truth is, I don't know."

Night had fully fallen now, and only pools of candlelight illuminated the room. Shadows contoured my mother's face. Through the open window came the lush orchestration of one of Sam's beloved operas. Mozart.

Mom continued. "Your grandmother was a healer, of course, like Toni and Jean," she added. "Aunt Beata had the gift of glamour—"

"Beata? Who's she?"

Mom looked confused for a moment. "My mother's sister. Beata. I forgot that you girls never met her. Or did you?"

Never met, never even caught a hint of her. "I haven't heard of her. At all."

"Of course you have," Mom said. "I'm sure we've talked about her." Mom looked at me strangely. "I haven't thought about Aunt Beata for years. Decades, even. And yet . . ."

"And yet what?"

"I feel sure there's something I'm supposed to remember." She shook her head as if to resettle the contents of her mind. "No. It's gone."

Something was interfering with my mother. Our protective circle should have kept out negative energy, which meant that whatever it was had come from inside her, not outside. "Tell me what you do remember about Aunt Beata."

For a moment, Mom didn't speak. I saw her thoughts gather from long-forgotten corners of her memory and coalesce into a whole. "She was called Beata—'blessed'—because she was born long after my mother when my grandmother thought her childbearing years were finished. She was only a few years older than me." Mom closed her eyes tightly and opened them. "It's starting to come back now. I'm remembering her."

"She was a witch, too." I posed this as a statement, not a question. If she was Grandma's full sister, she had magic. How much magic, I didn't know.

"Yes. She had glamour."

"Glamour" had come up in my grandmother's lesson on love magic, but I didn't know much about it. Mom must have seen my uncertainty.

"Glamour is about being able to entrance someone, gain their affection," she said. "If she put her mind to it, Aunt Beata could charm you, although 'charm' is too benign a description. In the wrong hands, glamour can bewitch crowds and even turn the fortunes of nations. Some of the world's most dangerous rulers were masters of glamour who could convince people that the most horrible of actions were justified—desirable, even."

The memory returned of the movie screen at the Empress and my grandmother casting a banishment spell. "How did Aunt Beata use it?"

"When I was a girl, I heard stories of her wrapping everyone from the plumber to her teachers around her little finger. She always got the best seat on the bus or the extra cream puff. Later, women stepped between her and their husbands. She had the gift of somehow appearing to be just what you wanted or needed. That's how glamour works."

I could see how this could be a dangerous gift if in the wrong hands—or a powerfully good one. Surely Mother Teresa had glamour. "Was she kind?"

Mom thought about this. "I don't know." She wrinkled her brow. "I'm thinking there was something about a baby. Something . . . no. I can't remember anything else."

Not a good sign. Why hadn't I heard of this aunt? "Her gift was glamour. What was her drive?"

Mom leaned back and a hand came up to flick a lock of hair between her fingers, a habit when she was deep in thought. "I'm not sure about that, either. When she left, I was pregnant with you and deep into my own world. After Dad died, Aunt Beata disappeared. Mom never talked about it. I guess I assumed she was off on her own adventures, and she slipped from my mind completely."

"So she may well be alive now. Somewhere. I bet I could track her down." I knew so few witches, that it was a shame to have another one roaming the planet who I didn't know.

"Presumably." A cloud settled over my mother's expression. I sensed her intuition had pinged, but I didn't know if she'd acknowledge it. Despite the rising heat, she rubbed her shoulders as if to warm them. "Something's wrong there."

"What do you mean?" I spoke quickly, to get a response before Mom retreated into her shell of "no magic, none of the time." "Could Aunt Beata somehow be behind the energy interfering with me?"

She inhaled and let it out slowly. "I doubt it. Why would she, after all these years? You'd better let her be. My mother wouldn't have cut off contact with her unless she had a good reason." Once more, her brow furrowed. "She never did mention her sister after she left. Never said a word. Except that last day."

There could have only been one last day—the day Grandma died. I was barely ten years old then, but with cut-glass precision I remembered her lying in her smooth cotton sheets, one of her ginger tomcats keeping vigil at her feet. A vase of sage branches was on her bedside table, and rain beat on the windowsills. Grandma's hand was dry as she clasped mine. Her lips formed words I didn't understand.

"What did she say?" I asked my mother.

"It was odd. She said, 'Remember my sister Beata?' When I nodded, she said, 'Forget her.'"

Outside, a crow cawed, and I shivered. All at once, the candles snuffed to black.

CHAPTER TEN

Mom left early the next morning with Emilio Landau for a day trip to the coast. He pulled his ivory Mercedes convertible into the library's driveway and politely shook my hand. I eyed the wicker hamper behind his leather seat. There had better not be a bottle of champagne in it.

"Nora?" He turned to my mother. "I hope you like champagne. Shall I put down the top?"

She giggled. My mother actually giggled. "That sounds great, thank you."

I watched them drive off, wind ruffling my mother's bob.

Inside the library, I grabbed my phone and dialed home. I was just about to hang up when my father answered. I pictured him at the landline on the kitchen counter, holding the headset to a jaw that could probably use a shave.

"Josie!" Dad might be absent-minded, but he truly did love his daughters. "How are things way out west?"

"Good." Hearing Dad's voice dispelled some of my irritation at Emilio Landau. "What are you working on now?"

I expected a wandering description of something like Danton's role in the French Revolution, abruptly shifting to a "Enough of this boring old stuff. How are you?" but instead he said, "I'm trying to heat up some lunch. Are you familiar with our microwave?"

"Dad, what's going on between you and Mom?"

Random beeps punctuated the background. Dad was clearly punching the microwave's controls. Although his office was a no-man's-land of stacked books and papers, he was generally tidy, and I pictured the clean coffeepot upturned on a dishtowel and the dishes put away.

"Come again?"

"You and Mom. Is anything going on that I should know about?" I glanced at the clock. I'd better get to opening the library.

Dad sighed. Here it came. "I guess I'll just have to make a sandwich."

"Dad. I asked you question."

"About your mother? Yes. No."

"Yes, no, what?" I asked.

"Is she all right? Your mother?"

"Why wouldn't she be all right?" Good grief. This was starting to sound like an Abbott and Costello routine.

"You asked about her. Nothing is wrong, is it? Toni keeps calling and leaving messages about her. I haven't had the chance to call her back."

This was going nowhere. I knew defeat when I saw

it. "Just checking in, Dad. See the 'minute' button on the microwave? Push it twice. That should do it."

I slipped my phone into my skirt pocket and hurried to unbolt the library's foyer door with its stained glass window. It wasn't often that patrons were waiting on the porch—regulars used the kitchen door and stopped for a cup of coffee on the way in—but I prided myself on punctuality. Next I unbolted the heavy front door to the warm summer morning, birds singing in the oaks and a sweet breeze. I checked the book return box.

I turned to reenter the library, and a flash of red near the front steps caught my eye. I leaned over the porch railing to see Benjamin Duffy's wife, Lucy, with her back to me, staring toward the river. Something about her posture—the dipped head, the lifeless hands—put me on alert.

"Lucy?" I said tentatively. "Are you okay?"

When she lifted her head, I breathed a sigh of relief. She would be grieving deeply. People had been known to hurt themselves.

"Are you all right? Would you like to come in?" I asked.

Seconds stretched to a minute. Lucy slowly turned toward me. "They have it all wrong."

"About what?"

Lucy's eyes held a wild look—wild yet exhausted. "About Benjamin. His death was no accident."

I ushered Lucy into the library and into my office. Once she was settled in the armchair, I brought her a glass of water and closed the door. The day's heat was rising, but with the window open to the river, the office was still blessedly cool.

"How do you feel?" I asked. "You're going through a hard time." Inadequate words, I knew. "Can I help?"

Lucy turned her gaze toward me. If the smudges under her eyes were any indication, she'd barely slept since her husband's death. Why was she here instead of home with family?

"I need help. Somebody's help," she said. "I knocked on the sheriff's door, but no one answered."

"Sam's at work." I took my desk chair and leaned forward. "Can I do anything for you?"

"People think . . ." She looked away and tried again. "People think Benjamin's death was an accident. That he was drinking and fell." She looked me in the eye. "It's not true."

So this was it, then. She was having a hard time accepting that her husband had relapsed, despite the evidence. "I'm sorry."

She pulled back. "You don't believe me, do you?"

"It's not my—"

"Like everyone else, you think he sat on that deck with a bottle of whiskey. You think he waited until I had to go into town, then started drinking." She shook her head vigorously. "No. It's not true."

"This whole situation is very hard on you."

"He was not drinking, not using. Don't you think I'd know?" A hand lowered to her belly, as if the idea nauseated her.

Rodney appeared in the office window and soundlessly dropped to my desk. He stood near me, his tail brushing my cheek.

"If it wasn't an accident," I said, "what happened?"

She drew herself up in the chair. "The only possible answer is that it was a setup."

She was clearly delirious. Her husband's death had pushed her over some emotional edge, and she wasn't able to think straight. We librarians were used to dealing with a wide range of patrons and needs, but I wasn't qualified for this.

"You don't believe me," Lucy repeated. "Benjamin was looking forward to living here again. You heard him at the estate sale. You were there. Benjamin missed Adam, and he even missed his father." The grimace that passed over her face revealed what she'd thought of that. "He wanted away from New York, away from his old life."

Yes, I remembered Benjamin saying so. I also remembered Lucy's reaction. "You weren't as happy about it."

She stared at me. An unkempt chunk of dark hair fell from behind an ear. "No, I wasn't. But I was happy about Benjamin finding himself again. I'd never seen him so hopeful. It was wonderful. And now . . ."

"To clarify," I said, "you believe your husband was murdered and it was set up to look like an accident." Maybe the shock of the bald statement would jolt Lucy back to reality.

She merely nodded.

"Why? Why would someone kill him?"

Eyebrows drawn, she stared at me. "How am I supposed to know?"

Only facts would dissuade Lucy now. The loss of her husband coupled with the suspicion of murder was too much for one person to handle. Add the hysteria fanned by anonymous letters and the resulting hotbed of drama, and anyone would start to suspect murder.

"Here's what we'll do." I turned to my computer to look up a phone number. "Your husband's body is with the medical examiner, right?" This was standard procedure for an unexpected death.

Lucy nodded.

"We'll call them and make sure they test his blood for alcohol—in cases like this, they usually do—and report to you on the results. If Benjamin had been drinking, we'll know it was a tragic accident. If not, well, the sheriff can take it from there." I handed Lucy the phone.

When she hung up a few minutes later, she was calmer. Still sad to her bones, but more collected. I waved goodbye to her from the library's porch. She said she was headed home for a shower and a nap.

Then I turned to my next order of business: tracking down Aunt Beata.

CHAPTER ELEVEN

I'd never before hesitated to see Sam, but I did to-night.

Our date almost didn't happen. I'd received a text from him during the afternoon, canceling our dinner plans. He'd said he had to work—at least, I thought he had. By chance I was trying to convince Rodney to come in, when I saw Sam pull up to Big House. At his greet-ing—a wide frown indicating happiness—I couldn't re-sist hurrying across the lawn to kiss him hello.

"Too bad you have to work tonight," I said.

His frown morphed to puzzlement. "I'm home for the day."

I pulled my phone from my pocket. "But I was sure . . ." No text. Had I imagined the whole thing? The memory surfaced of last night's talk with Mom and the dark energy that had seeped into my life. "Then I'll see you soon."

That was an hour ago. Mom was now ensconced up-stairs in her bed with a stack of novels. She said she had to "get her head on straight," and the books had decided to assist by supplementing her beach reads with self-help manuals.

Before I left, I went upstairs to say goodbye. Mom patted the mattress next to her as a signal to sit. The day was cooling, and a river-scented breeze ruffled the makeshift linen curtains.

"You'll tell him tonight, won't you, honey?" Mom had asked. "You need to let Sam know before he finds out another way."

I nodded. "It happened again. I thought he'd texted me to cancel tonight's plans, but he denied it. When I went to check the text, it was gone."

Mom pulled herself upright. "I don't like this."

"Me, neither. Although nothing dangerous has happened. Only small, annoying things." The books piled by Mom's bed held no answers. The books hadn't weighed in on the intruding magic at all. "I looked up Aunt Beata today. I couldn't find much beyond her birth certificate and some high school yearbook photos. She was a looker."

"She may have married and changed her name. She could be anywhere now. If she's alive, she'd be in her late fifties."

"I can't believe she's behind the force messing with me. What would she gain from it? In any case, I've already decided to tell Sam about being a witch. After that letter"—*I know your secret*—"I have no choice." I let my hands flop to the chenille bedspread. "I don't even know how to start. How did you tell Dad?"

Mom cleared her throat and busied herself straightening the books by her bed.

My jaw dropped. "You've never told him, have you?"

Mom's gaze swept the tower room before landing on mine. "Why should I?"

"Oh, Mom. I can't believe it. You haven't even dropped a hint? Not about Grandma? Or your own gift?"

"Gerard has other things to think about. Besides, you girls didn't show much aptitude for magic."

"What about me?"

This was a sore subject and one I'd only discussed with her once. The DNA lottery had awarded me the star-shaped birthmark on my shoulder, the sign I could marshal magic in a powerful way. After a vivid vision of my magic threatening my life, my mother convinced my grandmother to stem my power. That spell had snapped when I'd come to Wilfred, and I'd found myself dropped into a world I had no tools to manage. Fortunately, my grandmother had the foresight to prepare magic lessons for me. I had no other mentor. They had become my lifeline.

My mother raised her eyes to mine. "I did what I did to protect you." She laid a hand on my arm. "Which is what I'm doing now. If you want a future with Sam, you have to tell him about your abilities. With your father, it's different. You know how he is."

I did know my father. He loved us, but he might not notice if one of us turned into a unicorn. Unless that unicorn was a symbol on a Gobelin tapestry signifying something important to a period of French history.

"I still think you should be honest with Dad. Just because you didn't say anything earlier doesn't mean you can't now." Frustrated, I stood. "No wonder you're feeling alienated from Dad. You've kept something tremendously important from him. If he doesn't pay a lot of attention to you, it's because you've trained him to be that way by shutting him out. Why, today when I talked with him, he—"

"Josie! You called your father?"

"Why shouldn't I?" I folded my arms over my chest. My mother turned away.

"Mom, he's my father. I wanted to check in on him." When she didn't reply, I added, "You haven't even told him you're considering divorce, have you? You've kept your magic from him, and now this."

I expected my mother to be furious. Instead, she quietly picked at one of the bedspread's chenille rows and whispered, "It's too late to tell him about the magic. It's been too many years."

Now I was the one doling out the advice. "It's never too late." I moved to the door. "I have to go, meet Sam. If I can tell him I'm a witch, you can find a way to talk to Dad. No matter what happens, he needs to know."

Sam opened the kitchen windows to let in the cooler evening breeze while I piled the makings of a chilled *salade niçoise* onto a platter. In the corner of the kitchen, Nicky was stacking wooden blocks while Rodney groomed himself at the toddler's side. Sam sneezed, and I squeezed his arm. He was allergic to cats but, for my sake, welcomed Rodney.

I pondered my approach to telling him about being a witch. Maybe I'd chuckle and say, "You'll never believe it, but I'm actually a witch!" Or, I might take a more serious tack and sit him down. "Sam," I'd tell him, "you're an open-minded man, right?" Or I could feel him out. "Say, what do you think of magic?"

In the end, I punted. I'd wait until after dinner to tell Sam. Everything was better on a full belly, right?

Sam put Nicky to bed and we took our plates to the kitchen porch to watch the day slip into evening. The breeze off the river smelled sweetly of the cottonwood trees and shushed through their canopy as the light turned orange then pink then indigo.

"I saw Lucy, Benjamin Duffy's wife, today," I said.

Sam looked up from his plate with a vague frown. He knew me. He knew my tone of voice. "I heard she asked the medical examiner's office to call her with the results of his blood alcohol test. You didn't have anything to do with that, did you?"

I swallowed my bite of tuna and tomato. "She was so upset. So sure he couldn't have relapsed. If a blood test brings her peace of mind, that's not so bad."

I wasn't sure if he'd resent my meddling, and I relaxed when his face settled into a slight frown. He reached across the arm of his Adirondack chair to hold my hand. "You're a kind woman, Josie. I'm afraid she'll be disappointed, though. That railing—" He shook his head. "The railing was nearly rotted through. It's a miracle no one had fallen before. I'm afraid it was an accident."

Poor Lucy. I set my plate on the ground next to me, and Rodney nosed it for tuna scraps. "Any headway on finding who's been writing the poison-pen letters?" The memory of my own letter burned, reminding me I had to tell Sam my secret.

"Nothing. Really, there's not much we can do unless there's a threat or extortion." He set down his plate, too, and Rodney scampered over. "I doubt the sheriff's department would take it on, especially with our current workload."

"I don't like what the letters are doing to people."

"Neither do I." I couldn't draw out specific examples, but the feelings of doubt and suspicion were tangible. Formerly friendly people now avoided eye contact, and along Wilfred's streets, curtains were drawn. At the P.O. Market I saw neighbors actively turn their backs on each other, one man nodding over his shoulder with a comment about how "some people would do anything." Follow-up letters, if they came, would only deepen the rifts that were now forming.

I had to tell Sam about my letter and my secret. A lump thickened in my throat. *Just say it, Josie. Say it.*

"Is something wrong?" Sam asked.

I opened my mouth to speak, but the words wouldn't come.

"Did you get a letter, too?" he said.

Mute, I nodded.

He visibly relaxed. "So that's it. I could tell something was on your mind. I wouldn't worry about it. Someone is getting their jollies terrorizing people, that's all." He raised an eyebrow. "Although I can't imagine what they'd accuse you of. What did your letter say?"

I managed to choke out, "I know your secret."

"What secret? I don't keep any secrets from you."

"That's what the letter said. 'I know your secret.'"

Sam laughed. "That's a good one. What is it, Josie?

A secret baby? Nicky would like that. Second career as an international spy? Or maybe you write erotica on the side?"

His laughter should have been comforting. Instead, it irritated me, which loosened my tongue. "You don't think I have secrets? It just so happens I have a big one." As soon as the words left my mouth, I regretted them. Yes, I had come tonight to tell Sam I was a witch, but I hadn't intended it to come out like this.

To Sam's credit, he realized I was serious. "Let's go inside." He led me through the kitchen to the living room couch and sat me down. "You have something to tell me, don't you?"

"We were going to have dessert . . ." I said.

"It can wait." Sam's voice was gentle. Summer wind through the open window caught the curtains. Something new was blowing in. "What do you have to tell me?"

Say it, Josie. Tell him. Sam had enriched and deepened my world. He had opened up every dimension of me, and I had opened up to him—in every way except one. And it was a big one. Sam was a logical man. He had a softer side—I'd seen that often enough in how he cared for Nicky or dealt with a drunken patron at Darla's—but reason drove him. Telling him about my magic could sever our bond completely. He wouldn't believe me. Or, if he did, he wouldn't be able to accept it as a part of his life.

Yet, what choice did I have? For me, magic was a force stronger than the others. It wasn't simply something I did, it was something I was. I was a witch. Either he would accept that or reject it, but I wasn't going to hide my magic from him any longer.

I closed my eyes and willed the words from my lips. "I'm a witch."

I heard Sam's soft exhale. He eased me into his arms. "Of course you are."

I pulled away and opened my eyes. "I'm serious, Sam. I'm an actual witch."

He frowned in amusement. "Hmm."

"It isn't easy to admit. I—"

From the kitchen, Sam's phone rang. The phone he kept for work. Sam glanced at the clock on the mantel, then back at me. "You can ply your magical powers on me in a moment, Josie. I'd better take this. They wouldn't be calling so late without a good reason."

The sofa creaked as he rose. He disappeared into the kitchen and returned, frowning—happy—holding the phone. He answered the call, and his frown turned to a smile. Something was wrong. "I see. It's late now. I'll be in early to start the investigation." He hung up, then stared at the phone.

"What is it?" I asked.

His gaze shifted to me. "Benjamin Duffy. The medical examiner found no trace of alcohol in his body." He shook his head. "You could smell it on him, though."

"Oh no." My attempt to persuade Sam of my magic fell to the side.

Lucy had been right. Her husband's death had been no accident, merely designed to look like one. It had been a setup. It was murder.

CHAPTER TWELVE

"Is it always like this?" Mom asked.

She leaned back on my Victorian sofa with her cup of morning coffee at her elbow. Rodney lounged in the open window, his tail flicking the sill, and I sat legs drawn up in the armchair by the fireplace. As often happened, the books floated a quote to me, this one from Emily Dickinson. *"'The Sun—just touched the Morning; The Morning—Happy thing.'"* The poetry shelf was full of romantics.

"Always like what?" I said.

"You know—murder and poison-pen letters."

"The letters are new," I ventured.

Mom merely sighed.

I shook my head. "I don't know where it comes from. We're a quiet, friendly community. The town is small. People go way back together. If you buy cough drops at the P.O., by evening you'll have two casseroles and a homemade tea for colds on your porch."

I wasn't exaggerating. Until recently, Wilfred had

been shrinking in population, and there wasn't enough new blood to bring in trouble. Yet we somehow managed to experience more than our fair share of homicides.

"Murder sprouts from something—jealousy, greed, and anger, for instance. Secrets. It doesn't take a big city to drum those up." Mom set her coffee cup on the side table. "Speaking of secrets, you didn't tell Sam, did you?"

I'd come so close. "No. I mean, I told him I was a witch, but he thought I was joking. I didn't have time to explain myself before the medical examiner's office called about Benjamin Duffy. I'll try again." I thought about my anonymous letter—*I know your secret*—hidden at the bottom of my desk drawer.

We sat for a moment contemplating this, and a quiet thunder rumbled in the distance. A heat storm. They were rare in this part of the world but deadly and sparked lightning that could start wildfires.

"Do you . . ." I looked at my mother. "Do you have, you know, any intuitive feel about this situation? Either the letters or the murder?"

Mom studied the chipped bust of Emily Dickinson. "You know I don't do that."

"Not consciously, maybe not full visions, but I know you get hits sometimes."

Mom's gift of foresight had been locked up tighter than my poison-pen letter, but magic wasn't always so easy to hide away, unless bound by a spell. Even that had its weak spots. As much as she claimed to ignore her magic, Mom would have flashes of intuition that led her to avoid certain intersections when traffic was heavy or to cash in on a sale of pineapples, for example. If she'd chosen to embrace her gift, she could read circumstances like meteorologists read the jet stream.

Mom leaned back against the sofa's mohair cushion. "Just a sense of uneasiness. Something nasty is brewing." In other words, Mom refused to let loose her gift of foresight. Again, she sighed. "If only Gerard were here. He has such a logical mind."

"You miss Dad," I said.

"I didn't say that," she responded quickly to the accompaniment of a clap of thunder and flash of lightning. No rain.

Thinking of my father reminded me that I had yet to come clean with Sam about my witchcraft, and I needed to. Soon. Especially if a stranger was prepared to hold my secret as ransom. Then another thought rose. "You don't think the anonymous letters and Benjamin Duffy's murder are related, do you?"

Considering this, Mom raised then lowered an eyebrow.

"Wilfred's a small town," I added. "What are the odds of having both a poison-pen letter writer and a murderer at the same time? Could they be linked?"

Thunder rumbled, quickly followed by slashes of lightning.

"Nah," we said in unison.

That afternoon the sounds of story hour filled Old Man Thurston's office, now Children's Literature. Even the room's dark paneling couldn't dim the joy of kids pointing at the book Sherry held and singing responses. Throughout the rest of the library, books sighed happily and murmured, *"Choose me!"* from their shelves. The set of outdated encyclopedias—Roz had been at me for months to donate them—hummed in baritone as the Fletcher twins flipped through the volumes, pointing at illustrations of emus and B-17 bombers and reading entries aloud while summer air poured in from the French doors open to the garden. The heat storm had moved on, and the sky was delft blue.

This was how I loved to see the library. This was why I'd become a librarian. It was almost enough to make me forget about Benjamin Duffy's murder and the anonymous letters. Mirroring my mood, Rodney sat at my feet and flicked his tail against my ankles.

"What do you think, baby?" I asked him. "Should we see what kind of mess the kitchen is in?"

Today, Buffy and Thor sat at the long kitchen table. Thor squinted at a copy of *How to Win Friends and Influence People* while Buffy sorted the packets of ketchup and hot sauce that had been left in the refrigerator.

"Hi, Josie," she said.

Buffy generally favored T-shirts with princess or unicorn motifs, often in glitter, accompanied by a tutu that had seen better days. Today she had on an adult's petticoat that looked made to wear under a square dancer's skirt. She had pulled it up like an evening gown with the waist firmly safety-pinned beneath her armpits. Under the petticoat was her usual T-shirt and, I suspected, shorts, probably pink.

"Hello. Thor, isn't that book a tough read?" Thor

typically favored middle-grade fiction featuring super-heroes, although lately he'd been on a jag of classic comic books and a week earlier had followed me through the library discussing the plot of *Treasure Island*, his cape flapping behind him.

Thor had the courtesy to close his book before re-plying, but my guess is that it was less his manners than his lack of interest in Dale Carnegie's dry prose. "Ellie says it's a must-read for the successful ex-traprenuer."

"Entrepreneur," I said automatically. Then, "Ellie Wallingford?" What did an overeager majorette know about starting a business? Sure, her family ran a guest-house, but that didn't make any of them Warren Buffett.

"Ellie says Mr. Landau gave her business tips to help her earn money for majorette camp," Buffy said. "Say, could I take these packets? They're just cluttering the refrigerator."

"You can have half of them. Leave the rest for pa-trons." I suspected I'd see Buffy in the parking lot of Darla's Café that very evening pawning them off for a buck a packet to customers leaving with takeout. "Emilio Landau, huh?"

"Ellie says Mr. Landau told her you have to be ruth-less to be rich," Thor recited.

"Take nothing personally," Buffy added.

"Eyes on the bottom line," Thor said. "Creativity is king."

What this might mean for Buffy and Thor's money-making ventures alarmed me—not to mention the cor-rosive effect of lame clichés. They'd already run through a full menu of enterprises, from performing magic tricks to offering tours of Wilfred to selling photos taken with their grandmother's tablet. What would be next?

Rodney leapt soundlessly to the table and lay down. I'd long stopped trying to keep him off. He groomed a black velvet paw and looked at me as if daring me to order him to the floor.

"Grandma says we should be looking for the person writing those mean letters," Buffy said. "People would pay big for that."

I mentally applauded Patty's efforts to nudge Buffy and Thor's energy toward something useful. In fact, the more I thought about it, the better I liked it. "That's a great idea. I suppose it's too late to question Derwin." Derwin Garlington, Wilfred's mail carrier. "The last letters came—what?—three days ago?"

Thor had pierced a ketchup packet and was sucking it dry. He lifted his head long enough to say, "Oh, no. Grandma got another one this morning."

My head shot up. "More letters?"

"Sure." Buffy scooped the packets away from Thor. "Mrs. Littlewood got one. Duke did, too. Probably others."

It wasn't over. The letters continued. This time, I was sure, they wouldn't be simple allegations. They'd make demands. The letter writer was upping the stakes.

CHAPTER THIRTEEN

Buffy and Thor's announcement of a second round of letters proved to be accurate. I heard whisperings between patrons, saw accusing glances across the room, and once caught a glimpse of a letter slid from a pocket. So far, I hadn't received a follow-up letter of my own, but I'd held my breath when sorting that afternoon's mail.

Mona was the first to reveal the follow-up letter's demands. "They want twenty bucks," she told me. "Twenty dollars and they won't tell what happened when I rescued that kitten."

From the look of Rodney happily snoozing in her lap, whatever she'd done didn't translate into a universal grudge against cats. Knowing Mona, it had something to do with revenge on whoever had abandoned the cat. Rodney lifted his head and blinked at me with bliss.

"Did they tell you how to deliver the money?" I asked.

"Not yet." Mona continued her ministrations to Rodney, and he purred at a decibel-straining level. "I'm sure they will. Eventually."

Whatever was afoot, I needed to make my magic clear to Sam before someone else got to him first. My letter was different from the rest, and I feared its demands would be more severe. Every quarter hour or so, I wandered to the French doors opening to the garden separating the library from Big House and looked for Sam. He wasn't home yet.

The books confirmed whatever doubts I'd had about the damage the poison-pen letters wrought. Titles including *Forgive For Good*, *Forgive: How Can I and Why Should I?*, and *Toxic Family 101* rushed through my head. The feeling down at the café would be even worse. What was happening to the town I knew and loved?

Emilio Landau strutted into Circulation. "Good afternoon, Josie." Today he wore a cream linen suit elegantly wrinkled at the elbows and knees, but otherwise pristine. He smoothed his mustache with an index finger in a catlike gesture.

"Can I help you?" I might have asked more curtly than usual.

Behind Emilio Landau the stranger I'd seen at the café a few days earlier perused a shelf of periodicals. He turned his narrow face with its ratlike whiskers toward me. I hadn't even seen him come in. Who was he, anyway?

"That's quite a striking painting hanging over the foyer door," Emilio said. "Do you know its history?"

My heart warmed to this question. Maybe Emilio

wasn't so bad after all. I led him back into the atrium and we gazed up at the full-length portrait hanging over the entrance. "That's Marilyn Wilfred, the library's founder and the little sister of Thurston Wilfred, the man who established Wilfred and built the mansion."

Marilyn looked down at us with amusement. The portrait had been painted a century earlier in the mansion's atrium, next to the table that still held Lyndon's floral arrangements. Today featured a riot of dahlias that Lyndon had scavenged from the garden. In the portrait, the vase held trailing branches of purple clematis. Marilyn wore a beaded flapper gown and headband and rested a hand on an armchair. At her feet sat a black cat that could have been Rodney—if Rodney were now a century old.

"Nice work. Skillfully rendered. She looks nearly alive, this Miss Wilfred."

I smiled at the portrait. "She was a legend. Beloved, especially in her later years. People still tell stories about how she helped them pay vet bills or get through college. The library was a community center then."

He dropped his gaze to me. "Of course, there's not much market for portraiture unless the artist is well-known. Is your mother around?"

Fortunately—for me, if not for Emilio Landau— Mom was walking in the woods. She'd tucked a novel in her pocket and said she needed time to think. "She's out. Sorry I can't help you."

As he left, Patty entered. She turned to watch Emilio Landau, thumbs hooked on pants pockets, saunter through the atrium and cast his gaze up to the second floor. I swear Marilyn Wilfred narrowed her eyes at him from the painting.

"Can I help you?" I hoped Patty had stopped by to chat rather than search for yet another exercise book she'd peruse with a chocolate malted in hand.

"He looks familiar," she said.

"Emilio Landau? He has a certain style about him. You know, international bon vivant," I said. I hoped my tone didn't sound too nasty.

"He could be . . . no. Impossible," Patty said.

"Impossible, what?"

"Something is familiar about him from way back. It's that look. But what's a look?" She stepped closer. "My brain's somewhere else."

I let a few moments lapse without replying, hoping she'd elaborate. She didn't.

"Maybe I can help you find a book?"

Patty continued to stare toward the atrium. Eventually she returned her gaze to me. "What's happening in Wilfred? The whole town has lost its head."

"The letters," I said.

"Yes. I thought we were stronger than this." Patty perched on the corner of the circulation desk. Maybe it was my imagination, but she did seem to be more limber than usual. Perhaps the yoga DVDs she'd requested had been working.

"I've noticed," I said. "It's a nasty undercurrent. I can't put my finger on anything in particular, but I feel it." If emotion were a barometer, the needle had swung toward "storm warning." "Did you get a letter, too?"

"Two of them. The first was vicious, and Darla . . ." She didn't finish.

"What about Darla?"

"All I can say is this: If a few letters can tear Wilfred apart, what does that say for us?"

When I returned to my desk in Circulation, the rat-faced stranger had left. Hopefully he'd found what he'd been looking for.

As for me, I planned to learn all I could about Emilio Landau. Patty might be concerned about letters tearing the town apart. I was concerned about an oily art appraiser tearing apart my parents' marriage.

Emilio Landau's website was a static page featuring his name above the medieval eel I'd seen on his business card and monogrammed on his shirts. Below that was ART APPRAISER, SERIOUS INQUIRIES ONLY. They'd have to be serious, because he hadn't listed contact information. Despite sweeping the page with my mouse, nothing lit up as linked elsewhere. What kind of businessman had no way to contact him?

I scoured social media and came up dry. I was surprised. Emilio Landau was an unusual name, and I'd anticipated something—a photo caption at a social event, a business listing, anything. Lost in thought, I closed my laptop.

Something about Emilio Landau was not right. The problem was that I didn't know what it was.

CHAPTER FOURTEEN

After the bad feelings swirling through the day, comfort food at Darla's was just what I needed. Mom and I were gathering our purses for an evening at the café when we heard pounding at the library's front door. The library was closed for the day, and I'd pulled the curtains shut and turned off the lights. Although the summer evening outside was still light, the library was dim, the atrium lit by only the waning sun through the stained glass cupola.

Another volley of pounding sounded from downstairs. Mom and I exchanged glances. With the mood in Wilfred, the pounding could mean anything—and it was likely a bigger deal than an after-hours book return.

"I'd better check it out," I said.

"I don't like the sound of this." Mom grabbed the poker from the hearth and held it pointed side out. "I'm coming with you."

Rodney followed us down the service staircase to the ground floor. I crossed the atrium and threw open the bolt to the old mansion's heavy front door and stepped back so fast I bumped into my mother. Half of Wilfred must have been in front of the library, crowding the porch and spilling down the stairs to the front drive. What was this? Mom lowered the poker.

Ruth Littlewood stood in front. She raised her hand to silence the mob behind her. "We'll need use of the library tonight." Her words came as a demand, not a request.

"We're closed," I said.

"This is a town emergency. The café is too small for a meeting." She raised her chin. "As a trustee, I demand after-hours use of the library."

Ruth Littlewood was long retired as head of her family's vegetable canning outfit, but her skills as a CEO continued strong. After-hours library use was common, but usually requested well ahead of time to make sure someone—me, usually—was here to keep an eye on things and lock up afterward.

I glanced over Ruth Littlewood's shoulders at the people waiting to be let in. This was no meeting of the birdwatching society. Duke and Desmond, still sporting grease-stained fingernails from their latest project, stood at one edge giving a Tohler the side-eye. Patty had her back turned to Darla, who pretended to look anywhere but at her sister. Darla's husband, Montgomery, placed a comforting hand on his wife's shoulders. That they were both here meant the gathering was important enough to close the café. The knitting club, a raucous bunch but usually a united force, were scattered through the crowd refusing to make eye contact. This was bad.

"Okay." I stood aside and let Wilfredians, led by Ruth Littlewood, filter in.

Without speaking, the townspeople commandeered the atrium. The central table with Lyndon's artfully arranged dahlias was moved to the side. Chairs were carried in from everywhere—the kitchen, conservatory, and Popular Fiction—until the atrium was filled with armchairs and ottomans. It looked like a garage sale at a once-posh mansion.

Mom and I stood at the room's edge and watched. The books were quick to chime in with titles: *Resolving Conflict*, *The Anatomy of Peace*, *Nonviolent Communication*, *Getting to Yes*. They chattered helpfully, one book speaking low with a Freud-inspired accent.

Ruth Littlewood didn't need any of them to rally her troops. "Everyone, take a seat." She'd stationed herself at the head of the room, near the entrance to the kitchen.

Mom smoothed her hair, and I raised an eyebrow. Since when did she care so much about how she looked? Emilio Landau slipped in and took a seat toward the rear. Now I understood. Although I didn't know why he'd be here. Surely he hadn't received a letter? Another surprise attendee was the stranger I'd noticed earlier at the café and then this morning at the library. He stood against the wall behind Emilio.

"Thank you for coming tonight," Ruth Littlewood said. Even without a microphone her voice reverberated in the atrium. "Many of us here have received anonymous letters accusing us of various crimes." She paused as if waiting for confirmation. Although no one in the crowd nodded, the way people looked at their fingers or tilted their heads to examine the stained glass cupola was confirmation. "And some of you might have come from sheer prurience. Whatever the case, we are stronger than the letter writer. Instead of hiding in shame and casting nasty looks at each other, we must band together."

I scanned the room. Besides Emilio Landau and the stranger, the rest of the attendees were longtime Wilfredians. Neither Lucy Duffy nor Adam Duffy had shown up, but that was to be expected—they were in mourning. The Wallingfords weren't here, either.

Ruth Littlewood continued. "The letter writer will expect us to keep quiet. It's by exposing us that they expect to profit." The crowd, in fact, was very quiet. "But we will thwart them. We will be courageous. We will share our knowledge to find the perpetrator of these damaging messages. If we hide nothing, we can't be blackmailed."

This was a turn of events. I turned to Mom to get her read, hoping she wasn't hungry now that our trip to the café was off. She, in turn, kept glancing at Emilio Landau. Feeling my glare, she gave me a bare shrug.

Duke stood. "What are you saying, Ruth? You want us to tell everyone what was in those letters?"

"I'll tell you what was in them," a member of the knitting club said. "Lies."

Ruth held up a palm for silence. "Which would you rather have: a situation where you're hiding allegations"—here she cast a glance at the member of the knitting club—"and are at the letter writer's mercy; or one where you have the courage to reveal what's in the letter and are free?"

To this apparently rhetorical question, no one answered.

"Together, we can overcome this. We can show this . . . this *criminal* that we won't be victims of their greed. Am I right?" Ruth Littlewood scanned the crowd.

Heads nodded in return. Desmond said, "Hear, hear."

"Besides that, we might gather clues as to who this person might be. Now, who wants to go first? Who will reveal what was in their letter?"

Apart from the noise of shuffling feet and creaking chairs, the room was silent. People looked everywhere, except at Ruth Littlewood. I couldn't speak for anyone else, but there was no way I was sharing the contents of my letter. Rodney's tail switched in my peripheral vision. He'd settled under the table of dahlias to watch the show.

"All right," Ruth Littlewood said. "I'll start." She slipped an envelope from her satchel, which usually held a notebook and binoculars for birdwatching, and posed half-moon reading glasses on her nose. "My first letter is composed of letters and words clipped from a magazine and glued to the page. Much like yours, I assume?" She looked over her glasses at the crowd.

People in the room were willing to admit to that much. Here and there, heads nodded. This confirmed that my letter was different from the rest.

"It reads"—she shook the letter gently—"no salutation, by the way." She cleared her throat, and her voice trembled. My respect for her grew. "It reads, 'You regularly trespassed on the Tohlers' land and in doing so ruined the potato patch.'"

The Tohlers, who occupied a sizable block of seats, grumbled. One of the senior family members—there were so many Tohlers that I admit I didn't know his name—stood. "So that was you, was it? We have mouths to feed. We'd been counting on those fingerlings."

Ruth Littlewood lowered the letter. "Yes. It is true. I inadvertently destroyed your potato patch. I had spotted the broad-tailed hummingbird, and I needed to confirm it."

The senior Tohler sputtered. "A bird? You ruined a dozen dinners to look at a hummingbird?"

"The broad-tailed hummingbird is rarely seen in our part of the world. This information is a vital addition to—"

"It was just a bird!"

Ruth Littlewood stood straighter. "I am truly sorry. I've arranged to have one hundred pounds of assorted potatoes delivered to your house this week."

To this news, the senior Tohler sat, his expression surprised and softened. His wife stood. "Ruth, that was years ago. We'd long forgotten the potato patch. Please don't go to the trouble."

Ruth Littlewood wasn't given to overt displays of emotion. She fixed her gaze on the second envelope in her hand. "Nonetheless, the transgression was mine, and I wish to make it right. You can always donate what you don't need to the food shelter." She slipped the second letter from its envelope. "Which makes this letter moot. Let me read it. 'Unless you agree to pay twenty dollars, your sins will be revealed.'"

"Does it say how to pay?" I asked from the sidelines. "We might catch the letter writer that way."

"No. No instructions. I assumed those were to follow."

Twenty dollars wasn't a lot of money. The potatoes had surely cost Ruth Littlewood more. Once again I wondered why the letter writer didn't fix on a way to pay. Sending a follow-up letter opened up the letter writer to another chance to be discovered. The whole situation was odd.

"Who else wants to share their letter?" Ruth Littlewood asked.

Duke looked around and, with reluctance, stood. "Thank you, Ruth, for your bravery. I'll go next. I fished in the millpond without a license. Not that I caught anything. There, I admit it." He sat.

Slowly and then quickly, the floodgates opened. Over the next hour, Wilfredians confessed to everything from not cleaning up after their dog to "borrowing" tomatoes, to using outdated coupons at the P.O. Orson admitted to watering down a few of his patrons' drinks at the tavern, but only those he knew had overshot their limits. Wilfredians followed their confessions with promises to make good.

I learned a few things about goings-on at the library, too, and made a note to check a folio of plays for a melted bonbon in its pages and to replace a book about Boston terriers that had had a photo of a puppy removed to adorn a teenager's bedroom. That teenager was now grown up with children of her own.

What these transgressions had in common was that they were minor and committed long before. The poison-pen letter writer must therefore be a longtime Wilfredian. Other than that, I was stumped. I saw nothing else linking them.

At last the room was calm, and a feeling of goodwill had even descended. While people talked, I opened the French doors in the rooms surrounding the atrium and lifted the conservatory's ceiling vents. The room was cool and peaceful, and the day's heavy atmosphere of shame and suspicion was lifting. Here and there people even laughed and hugged.

Only Darla and Patty refused to speak to each other. They stood on opposite sides of the atrium. When Patty cast glances toward Darla, Darla pointedly looked away. What could be going on there?

Ruth Littlewood again stood. "If everyone is feeling unburdened, we can continue. We have accomplished step one—we have defanged the writer of these letters. This person cannot get money from us if we have nothing to hide. They will understand it is fruitless to write further letters."

In the audience, heads nodded. Emilio Landau watched in amusement, crossing one linen-clad leg over the other. The stranger behind him shifted on his feet.

"Step two is to unmask this person who has created so much animosity between us."

One of the members of the knitting club stood. "How do you propose to do that? The letters are anonymous. There's nothing exceptional about the paper."

Wilfred's mail carrier Derwin Garlington stood next.

"No clues at the post office. The letters were all posted in Forest Grove on the same day."

Ruth Littlewood nodded. "To note: First, the letter writer has access to at least one old magazine and a glue stick."

"Possibly more than one glue stick," Duke added. "There's what? Two, three dozen letters?"

"One or more glue sticks," Ruth Littlewood amended. "As for the deeds the letter writer cites, they all took place years ago. Some even decades. Is this correct so far?"

Not so for me, I thought. I'd lived in Wilfred less than two years. My letter writer was someone else, someone potentially more sinister. The memory returned of the deadened fruit, the images on the tattered movie screen, candles extinguishing on their own—worse, the energy that had weighed so heavily on my own just the other night, rendering me nearly inert.

Ruth Littlewood continued. "The question is, who would have known these secrets?"

No one responded.

"Mona," Ruth Littlewood said. "When you saw Mr. Dalton yell at those kittens and consequently put sugar in his gas tank, who did you tell about it?"

Mona, a sleeping puppy in a knit sweater on her lap, looked startled. "No one. I didn't tell a soul."

"You must have," Ruth Littlewood replied. "Otherwise, how would the letter writer have known about it? Think back. Did you write about it in a diary? Tell your best friend?"

Mona cupped her palms around the puppy. "It was so long ago. I guess . . . I was ashamed, you know."

Several of the audience members nodded in sympathy.

"Maybe I mentioned it to Linda Tohler."

I'd never met Linda Tohler—she'd moved to California before I'd arrived in town. I'd heard about her love of animals, though. Stories still circulated about the goat that had given birth in her family's guest room without her mother's okay.

"Who else?" Ruth Littlewood said. "Did any of the rest of you tell Linda?"

Mrs. Tohler stood. "Honestly, Ruth. Linda has lived in Fresno for years, and she's making a perfectly good living as a court reporter. She is not blackmailing our neighbors."

The two women had a staring match for a moment. Ruth Littlewood relented. "Point well taken." She drew a long breath, and we could practically see the wheels spinning in her head. "We must formulate a plan to identify the writer of these anonymous letters. Do you agree?"

Cheers sounded throughout the atrium. Ruth was good. I couldn't wait to see what she would come up with.

"Therefore," she said, gaze lifted toward the ceiling, "I propose that our librarian, Josie Way, investigate."

CHAPTER FIFTEEN

When Mrs. Littlewood made her proclamation, I'd been studying the crowd, calculating how long it would take me to put everything back where it belonged.

"What?" I said, standing away from the wall where I'd leaned.

"I nominate you to find out who has been writing these filthy letters."

Heads swiveled toward me. A few nodded.

"But I don't—"

"Who will second the nomination?" she asked.

"I will," Duke said, likely because he was more titillated by my panicked expression than because he was convinced I could root out the letter writer.

"But this isn't a voting body. You have no authority—" I began.

"All in favor, say aye," Mrs. Littlewood said, and a chorus of ayes went round the room. "Any nays?"

"I say nay," I responded quickly. "Why me? What makes you think I can find the anonymous letter writer?"

Ruth Littlewood, clearly satisfied with a good evening's work, pulled up a Victorian side chair and sat. "It's obvious." When I stared back blankly, she continued. "You are a librarian and therefore an expert at research, am I right?"

"Some sorts of research, I mean I—"

Apparently I wasn't destined to finish a sentence tonight. Mrs. Littlewood leaned back. "When Junior Milchman needed to find out what to feed his budgie, you provided him with a complete diet plan."

"That was a budgie. This is something completely different," I pointed out.

Mrs. Littlewood held up a hand. "And when Marge Brucker was tracking down her family tree? You had the smarts to look at her great-grandfather's bequests for hints as to who her real uncle was."

That had been a feat, I had to admit. Marge had heard rumors that her unusually dark-eyed uncle had a different father than her grandfather. Yet the uncle had been raised as one of the family. Marge had sat in the library's Local History section, unsure where to start, when I'd heard a family history whisper *Start here. Legacies*. Tracking wills, then ordering a few DNA tests had proven Marge's uncle was directly related to a farmer in Gaston.

"Besides that," Mrs. Littlewood continued, "you're one of the few among us who hasn't received a letter. You have no motivation but Wilfred's public good."

I struggled to keep my expression neutral. I had certainly received a letter, but it was increasingly clear it had another author.

"I'm right, am I not?" she pressed.

I couldn't lie, but I definitely didn't want to get into details. It was fine for Madeline Carson to admit to swindling the P.O. of fifty cents for using an expired coupon, but I didn't even want to imagine what might happen if my witchcraft were made public. "A letter like these didn't arrive for me," I finally said. That much was true.

"Then you have no ulterior motive, except to foster the peace and well-being of Wilfredians," Ruth Littlewood concluded.

"Unless she wrote the letters herself," Sherry, head of the knitting club, said.

I looked at the people gathered in the atrium. Surely no one suspected me? I wouldn't have to prove myself innocent, would I?

The room erupted in laughter, eliciting a bewildered smile from me, too. Apparently the idea that I'd mastermind a poison-pen letter campaign was a good joke.

However, I wasn't ready to relent just yet. Despite remembering Sam's doubt about opening a case against the anonymous letter writer, I asked, "What about the sheriff's office? Shouldn't law enforcement investigate this?"

"What? Investigate letters about misdeeds several years old asking for piddling amounts of money?" Ruth Littlewood again stood. She'd clearly seen my comment coming and had prepared her rebuttal. "The cost of these letters isn't measured in the paltry sums they demand. It's in the bad feelings and suspicion they've engendered." She cast a meaningful glance first at Patty then at Darla, who stood at opposite sides of the atrium, facing away from each other. Whatever the letters had stirred up for them cut more deeply than trampled potatoes and outdated coupons. "The sheriff's office would laugh at us. It will take us to untangle the damage done." She squared herself against me. "So, what do you say, Josie? Can we count on you?"

Everyone in the room—including Patty and Darla—turned toward me, awaiting my response. Even my mother tilted her head in my direction.

The need for justice was in my DNA, and the matter of the poison-pen letters did call to me. I remembered Sam's assertion that the sheriff's office could do little. Beyond that, I had a more selfish reason. In investigating the letters, maybe I could find out who had written my letter and what it was they knew. From the amused set of my mother's lips, I could see she'd already anticipated my response.

"Yes," I said. "I'll do it. I'll find out who's been writing these letters."

After the crowd had left and chairs were put away, Mom and I went upstairs to my apartment's kitchen. Although Darla had announced the diner would reopen for the night, neither of us could face more people. Besides, we had a lot to discuss.

Mom set to work making grilled cheese sandwiches,

and I watched her from the tiny kitchen table, Rodney in my lap. There was something comforting about Mom's efficient movements as she prepared dinner. The clink of the skillet on the stove, the sliding of the mustard jar from the refrigerator, the even slices of cheese laid on bread calmed me.

"Now what?" I asked, my hand on Rodney's silky back.

"Pickles," Mom said. "If you have them."

"Not the sandwiches, the poison-pen letters. How am I supposed to find out who wrote them?"

Mom's motions slowed. I hoped she was having a vision, but given her stubbornness about not tuning in to her magic, it was unlikely. "We need to read as many of the letters as we can."

"To look for common threads," I added. Something in the transgressions recorded or in how the letters themselves were worded could point to their author. Besides, our investigation might wrench my mother's thoughts from Emilio Landau. My thoughts drifted to Darla and Patty, sisters unwilling to talk to each other. The sooner these letters were cleared up, the better.

"We could look at who hasn't received letters, too," Mom said.

"You think the anonymous letter writer wouldn't have received one?"

"Not that." As often happened, Mom and I had the same thought. "It's likely they did write themselves a letter."

"As cover," I said.

Mom slid the sandwiches from the skillet onto a cutting board and sliced them on the diagonal. This was so much better than going to the café. Despite the letters and Benjamin Duffy's murder, I felt myself relax under my mother's care.

"As I said, we'll need to see, firsthand, as many of the letters as we can." She rested a sandwich in front of me. Rodney hopped to the floor. "Would your magic resonate with the text?"

"It might," I said. "Maybe I could catch a common voice."

She nodded. "We see the letters, we note similarities and differences, and we talk with the people who received them. Then we take it from there."

I loved this talk of "we." "Mom, I'm so glad you're here."

She pulled out the chair across from me and lifted half a golden sandwich. "Thank you, honey."

"No one else's grilled cheese comes close to yours." The sandwich was perfect. Crispy, buttery bread, melting cheddar, the bare tang of mustard, and a slice of pickle.

"I have an idea," she said.

"What?"

"Maybe Emilio can help."

I set down my sandwich. "Why?"

"He has an enterprising way of looking at things. He might have good insight."

"Mom, I didn't want to say anything, but there's something suspicious about him. I looked him up online, and barely anything showed for Emilio Landau. He doesn't even have contact info on his web page." I watched my mother, but she didn't even flinch.

"Why should he? He's retiring. I told you that. Why not put Emilio's perspective to use here?"

My appetite was ruined. "Dad has good perspective, too."

"Josie, your father isn't here, is he?"

Then I understood. It was time to call Toni again, and this time not just to check in on Dad. We needed him in Wilfred, and stat.

As soon as Mom was tucked into bed and safely out of earshot, I called Toni. It was three hours later on the East Coast, but I didn't care.

"Hello? Josie?" came Toni's groggy voice. "Is everything okay?"

"Why haven't I heard from you about Dad?" I asked.

"Just a minute while I take the phone into the other room." Mattress springs creaked in the background. Then, "Do you know what time it is?"

"Two in the morning," I said promptly. "And getting later. Hopefully not too late to save Mom and Dad's marriage."

A windy sigh traversed the nearly three thousand miles between us. "I've left Dad messages. Once I even got him on the phone, but he completely blew off my questions about him and Mom. What else can I do?"

"You can visit him. Demand answers."

"Josie, I have a job. A kid. A husband. I have groceries to buy and a daughter to potty train. Driving across town to give Dad marriage counseling takes time, and I don't have it. That's assuming he'd listen at all."

I tapped a foot in frustration. "Oh, he'd listen all right. He probably needs someone to show him how to operate the washing machine. I imagine he has quite a backup of dirty laundry by now."

"Maybe Mom and Dad need to work it out on their own. They're adults. Their marriage isn't our business."

"What?" I couldn't believe what I was hearing. "You'd let them separate just like that? You know what a mistake that would be. They're made for each other."

From the other end of the line I heard a voice—my brother-in-law—then Toni's reply. "It's okay, honey. It's Josie. Nothing urgent."

"Nothing urgent? Only a threat to a loving bond formed over decades." Didn't she get it?

The magic that connected us sparkled even over geographical distance. Toni had heard my unspoken question. "I understand your panic, and I've done what I can do here. Why don't you work on Mom? You have her one-on-one."

"I've tried." Toni's point was well taken. If I couldn't convince our mother to give Dad another chance, why should I expect Toni to accomplish the same with Dad?

"There you go, then," Toni said. "I'll call Dad one

more time tomorrow, but that's it. We need to leave them to work out their own business."

I hated to admit it, but Toni was right. My chest felt hollow as I told her so.

"Good night, Josie."

"Good night." It took me a few seconds to press "end," but at last I did.

CHAPTER SIXTEEN

The next morning was a workday, which meant I couldn't wander Wilfred to buttonhole people who'd received letters. Mom had a solution.

"Ruth Littlewood likes to take charge, doesn't she?" Mom had asked.

"You saw it last night." Normally, Darla would have taken the reins on the poison-pen letter issue, but she had been unusually quiet.

"Why don't we ask her to line up letter recipients at the library? That way you can interview them but not miss work. Plus, everyone will see that you're taking your assignment seriously."

A telephone call later and Mrs. Littlewood had organized short appointments throughout the day, giving me ten minutes an hour to conduct library business "like a shrink," she'd said. With Roz as backup, I hoped to collect enough information to get some idea about the person writing the letters.

Of course, I wondered about Sam. He'd been clear

that the sheriff's department wouldn't take up the case—especially while there was a murderer to pursue. Would he begrudge me our investigation? And how about my confession that I was a witch? He'd laughed it off, and I hadn't had time to explain. I'd have to re-visit that conversation. Soon.

However, first the matter at hand. Mom led Duke into Circulation and pointed him to the chair across from my desk.

"Better make this fast," he said. "A leaky window in the break room at the P.O. needs fixing."

"What's the rush?" I said. "It's August. It won't rain for another month, at least."

Duke plopped into the chair, eliciting groans from its frame. "Space is tight. They use the break room as backup produce storage. Got to keep it cool."

I pulled up a pen and fresh notebook. "Did you bring your letter?"

"Right here." He drew a much-folded paper from his back pocket and leaned forward to smooth it on the desk. A few of the glued-on words had fallen off, but otherwise it looked like other letters I'd glimpsed.

The murmur of numbers led me to flip the letter over to see rows of figures. "What's this?"

"Desi and I were playing cribbage. I needed some-thing to keep score on."

Clearly, evidence would not be pristine. Fine. I'd work with what I had. The letter read, *You fish without a license. What would others think? You will pay.* The spelling and grammar were good. The letters were glued in relatively straight lines and nicely centered. Someone had spent time on this.

"Did you keep the envelope?"

"Nope." Duke leaned back in his chair again. Rodney hopped to the chair's upholstered back and settled near Duke's head.

"Was there anything unusual about it?"

He shrugged. "No return address. Naturally." He straightened. "There was one thing. It was addressed to 'Duke.' No last name."

Either the letter writer assumed everyone knew Duke—very possible—or didn't know his last name.

My thoughts were interrupted by a little girl. She smiled, showing missing top front teeth. She clutched a book with a tiger on its cover. Soft growls and roars wafted from its text. "Do you have anything else with cats?"

Where was Roz? She was supposed to take care of patrons while I was interviewing people who'd received letters. And where was the girl's mother?

The girl fixed her stare on Rodney. "Cat," she said and charged toward the chair. Rodney jumped down and dashed out the door, the girl on his heels.

"Liza! Where are you?" came a woman's voice from the atrium.

I returned my attention to Duke. "Do you really fish without a license?"

"That's the thing," he said. "Only a few times, early one season, in the millpond. I was trying to replicate Darla's creole trout recipe, and I didn't have time to get into town for a license. That was a long time ago, though."

A long time ago. I paused, pen above my notebook. "How long?"

"Eight, nine years. Maybe longer. Ask Darla when she first ran the trout special. That'll tell you."

I tapped the pen on paper. Whoever wrote the letters had been in Wilfred for a while. "Did you tell anyone about it? About fishing without a license, that is?"

"Maybe. Who can say? I paid for a license later that season. If I had anything to say about the trout at all, it would have been not to leave out the hot paprika. If whoever wrote this letter thinks I'll pay twenty bucks to keep it secret, they're nuts." He produced a second letter from his shirt pocket. "Extortion."

This letter was similar to the first, except that it was more quickly produced and was a clean demand for twenty dollars "to keep your sins quiet."

Duke rose. "If that's all, I'll be moving on."

"May I keep the letters?"

"Knock yourself out," he said.

The rest of the interviews followed a similar pattern. Besides last night's confessions, I added unpaid library fines (admitted with downcast eyes), dogs running free, a stolen Sunday paper, chewing gum that had been inadvertently added to a grocery checkout without being paid for, and cheating on a spelling test. All of these had follow-up letters demanding twenty dollars.

My last two interviews were with Darla and Patty. Ruth Littlewood had had trouble bringing Patty in. However, turning down Ruth's command was as useless as smoking a cigarette in a hurricane, and Patty had eventually relented. Darla had refused outright, saying if I wanted to talk with her I could find her myself.

By the time Patty arrived, Roz had closed the library. I kept the French doors open behind me for the warm breeze and scent of cut grass. Faraway yodels drifted up from the retreat center. Some Wilfredians had complained about the workshop—saying there should be a ban on yodeling and, after a poorly received retreat earlier this summer, barbershop quartets—but I liked it. Soon Sam would be arriving home, and I half listened for the rumble of the sheriff's department–issued SUV.

For now, though, I was tired. A day of work uniting people with books they loved filled me with energy and satisfaction. Talking with townspeople about secrets they'd rather forget drained me. The discord between Patty and Darla, however, was intriguing. Whatever it was, it was deeper and more insidious than the parade of petty sins I'd listened to all day.

Patty stood warily at the doorway at Circulation. "You wanted to talk?"

She knew what this was about. I stood. The workday was over. "Should we sit in the conservatory? Lyndon lifted the roof windows before he left."

I led the way. Mom was already there and had arranged three chairs and a side table next to a potted banana tree. She'd also brought down the box of chardonnay I kept in my upstairs refrigerator for Lalena's weekly dinner-and-bath nights—her trailer's tub was too small to be comfortable, and the library was home to a mammoth clawfoot bathtub. Mom might not have fully embraced her gift of foresight, but she did let hints of it leak through.

Patty didn't seem surprised at the wine or my mother's presence. She poured a generous measure and lowered herself into the chair near a rack of orchids. The air here was balmy and moist. If it weren't for the fir trees outside, we might have been on the patio of a hotel in the Bahamas.

Patty drained her glass. The side table jiggled as she slammed it down. "I have nothing to say."

Yet she was here. Mom pushed a plate of crackers and cheese toward Patty, and, without looking, Patty scooped a cracker into her mouth.

I opened my notebook, prepared to launch into the "when did you get your letter" and "tell me about this secret" speech I'd been making all day, but Mom warned me off with a stern glance. She lowered her eyes to my notebook, and I closed it. I returned her gaze with a questioning look of my own. She raised her chin. Message received. I put the notebook away. Mom would handle this one.

Mom's stern look melted into pure sympathy. "You received one of the letters."

Patty seemed briefly befuddled. A tear appeared at the corner of one eye.

I was used to Mom's searing gazes. When she looked at you—really looked at you—you couldn't help but wonder if she could read your thoughts. With her daughters, she definitely could. If she put in an effort, strangers wouldn't escape her, either. I watched Patty. How would she respond?

She clearly felt both Mom's insight and sympathy. "Yes."

Mom let a moment pass as she played with the stem of her wineglass. She hadn't taken more than a sip. Wise. The wine was pretty awful. "Maybe," she said softly, "you thought it had all been forgotten. You'd locked it away in your memory."

Patty burst into tears. "I never meant to hurt her. I only wanted her to be happy."

Patty had done something to wound her sister. Again I opened my mouth to ask for details, but Mom's sharp glance shut me down.

Mom slid her wineglass to the side and leaned forward, clasping her hands together on the table. "If you could tell your sister something, if she'd listen to you, what would you say?"

Man, Mom was good. I turned toward Patty for her reply.

Patty studied a crease in her jeans as if it were a map of the world. She drew a long breath. "I'd tell her I love her."

Mom nodded in encouragement.

"She always chose the wrong fellow." Now Patty's voice picked up force. "Always. They saw Darla's strength and figured they could leach off of her."

Before last year's marriage to Montgomery, Darla had had her share of husbands. I didn't know the details, but occasionally I'd catch word of "Troy the gambler" or "Lucky," who had an eye for the ladies and, despite his name, was unlucky enough to get caught. It didn't surprise me that a lazy man with enough enterprise to latch onto a powerful woman would focus his attention on Darla. She was strong, ran a successful café, and could seemingly manage the entire community's ills, from heartbreak to the common cold. Her husbands would have little more to do than relax and enjoy the ride. Darla had deserved better, and she'd found it in Montgomery.

"You thought you could help," Mom said.

"I had no idea it could backfire like that."

Backfire? I waited for Patty to continue. Mom had already made it clear I needed to keep my trap shut, but the suspense was killing me.

"Tell me more." Mom's voice was like the fabled snake charmer, and Patty's confession was the cobra.

"It was years ago."

Mom nodded.

"Darla was such a good sister, a good friend. She's only a couple of years older, but she cared for me like a mother. She cooked—of course—and read me the best bedtime stories, all from the same book." A faint smile played on Patty's lips. "Each time she picked up the book, it was a different story, usually a love story with a movie star or king. Sometimes lions or piranhas."

Darla was dyslexic. It didn't surprise me that she might invent stories rather than read a book. Neither did it surprise me that they were good ones. The books sighed *ooh* and *ahh*.

"At last, a real nice man was interested in Darla. She seemed to like him, too. He was terrific. He even had a job." Patty's glance from Mom to me said everything that needed to be said about this wondrous anomaly. "He simply needed a bit more encouragement."

Mom's gaze was focused. "So you provided it."

Patty collapsed against the chair. "I wrote him a note. A short one. I left it under his windshield wiper." Mom handed her a tissue, and Patty wiped her eyes. "Darla saw me. I didn't know it until later. She read the letter."

"And thought you were making a move on her boyfriend," Mom finished.

Patty nodded and resumed staring at her lap. "She was furious."

I sat back. There had to be more to this story. Obviously, they'd made up. The letter and the man were long behind them, and in my time in Wilfred I'd known Patty and Darla as loving sisters who joked and fiercely supported each other. I exchanged glances with my mother.

"That wasn't all, was it?" Mom asked.

All at once, Patty drew herself together. "I've told you all you need to know. The letter arrived last week, and the follow-up letter demanding twenty dollars came yesterday."

"Do you have the letters with you?" I asked. She was hiding something—or maybe she herself didn't understand why her letter had sparked such a strong reaction in Darla.

"Burned them," Patty said. "Filthy things."

She wasn't going to tell us the rest of the story. The letters had awakened something, though, and reopened the old rift between the sisters. Did Darla hold the rest of the story?

"Thank you for the lovely refreshments," Patty said sweetly. "I'd best be going now. Good luck with your inquiries." She stood. "Oh, and you might think about upgrading your wine—this stuff is foul."

CHAPTER SEVENTEEN

"Something about Patty's letter isn't right," I told Mom as we walked down the hill to the café. Last night's dinner of grilled cheese sandwiches was wonderful, but after listening to a blizzard of petty offenses, we deserved a good meal. Besides, Darla was working tonight. She was the one person I hadn't yet talked with, and, after Patty's story, the one I wanted most to hear.

"I agree," Mom said. "If she and her sister had already resolved this issue, why are they upset about it now? If I'm not mistaken, Patty is as bewildered as we are."

"Bewildered and hurt," I added.

"The letter had something more," Mom said. "I'm sure of it."

The sun hovered on the horizon, spilling light and warmth on the valley like an overturned margarita. The café's parking lot was full, and the café itself, when we entered, held a note of calm it had been missing lately. Last night's meeting at the library had cleared the air. That didn't mean conversation was all sweetness and light. I heard "Benjamin Duffy" mentioned at one table and "murder" at another.

Lalena waved from the counter. Ian Penclosa was wheeled up next to her. "Learn anything yet?"

"It hasn't even been a day," I said. Lalena's offense, besides being related to sheriffs with a weakness for attractive female drivers exceeding the speed limit, had been telling her third grade teacher she was psychic. Lalena had clung to this claim long enough to earn income reading palms and communicating with passed loved ones. She hadn't even bothered to deny the claim when she'd dropped off her letter with me this morning.

We found a table on the patio, and one of the multitudes of Tohler teenagers filled our water glasses almost instantly.

"Gumbo special," she said, dropping menus at a nearby table that had just settled. "With local shrimp and cherry tomatoes from Farmer Ted's garden."

"We'll take two," I said. "Mom, trust me, you'll love it. Christine"—I took a chance on the server's name. The Tohler girls looked so much alike—"could you ask Darla to stop by when she gets a minute?"

"Cindy," she said. "Christine is home packing for college. Sure, I'll let Darla know. She's busy tonight, though."

Christine—er, Cindy—disappeared into the café. Waiting for Darla wouldn't be a trial. It was a beautiful night. The breeze over the meadow behind the café and trailer park carried the scent of dried grass and the cool millpond as well as faint echoes of yodelers. And for once, even with an unsolved murder in our midst, the atmosphere was relaxed. Except, I noted, for Adam Duffy, picking at his dinner a few tables away. And Ellie Wallingford, walking up main street twirling her baton while looking daggers at the café.

"Mom, will you excuse me a moment?" I folded my napkin on the table and made my way to Adam Duffy. I felt awful for him. His brother had been murdered, and not long after his father's death. That thought led me to look for Lucy. Unless she was on the café's tavern side, she wasn't here tonight. "Adam? I want to tell you how sorry I was to hear about Benjamin."

He looked up at me with eyes that had clearly not seen much sleep, and his skin was grayer, more translucent. This is how he will look as an old man, I thought. A paperback thriller lay by his plate. From the urgency of the novel's muted gunfire and squealing tires, it was trying and failing to tempt him to open it.

"I heard you're following up on the anonymous letters," he said. "I didn't get one."

"You have more important matters to worry about," I said.

He dropped his gaze to his plate of shrimp and grits, which had been moved around but left largely uneaten.

"Would you like to sit with my mother and me? Maybe you'd rather not be alone right now."

"No, thank you. I'm not fit for anyone's company. I only left the house so Lucy could be alone."

My heart went out to him, but there was nothing I

could do to ease his mind. I returned to my table to find Darla dropping off our specials.

"I heard you wanted to talk to me?" Darla spoke to me, but she looked elsewhere, likely scanning the patio for empty plates and unfilled water glasses. The café was busy tonight.

"I wondered if I could talk to you about the poison-pen letter you received?" I asked.

Her attention shot to me. "That's none of your business."

I sat back. Darla, although often brusque, was rarely rude. The look in her eyes was more than anger, though. It was hurt. "Nothing personal. I'm collecting information about the letters to track down the person who wrote them."

Without responding, Darla crossed the patio in a few steps and disappeared into the café.

I cocked my head at my mother. "I don't get it."

Mom's gaze was still fastened on the door to the dining room. "One thing's for sure. She's not going to tell us anything."

Darla would be at the café for the rest of the evening. "There's one person who'll know what was in that letter. Her husband, Montgomery."

By the time we left the café, night had fallen. Moths buzzed near the mercury lights over the gravel parking lot, and crickets chirped from the meadow. The summer air was soft as Rodney's belly. For the thousandth time, I was so grateful to live in Wilfred. Even with the letters—and Benjamin Duffy's murder.

Darla and Montgomery lived in one of the Magnolia
Rolling Estates' nicest homes, which made sense since
Darla owned the trailer park. Mom's gaze swiveled
right and left as she took in the neat double row of mo-
bile homes, each parked at a precise angle and individ-
ually landscaped, from Lalena's tangle of roses and
sign proclaiming PALM READINGS to Ian Penclosa's
home, rented from Duke, with its manicured lawn and
tidy tool shed. Judging from the choir of voices ema-
nating from Ian's home, it was now full of rare books—
a notable change from the galloping horses and chaste
sighs I'd caught from Duke's favored Westerns and
Amish romances.

"This way," I told Mom and pointed to the double-
wide glowing with warm light. Through the screen
door I saw Montgomery in his recliner, a book in his
lap and reading glasses perched on his nose.

He rose before I could rap on the screen door's aluminum frame. "Josie, a pleasure to see you. This must
be your mother. We've heard so much about her."

Montgomery's voice flowed like a seductive mix of
bourbon and molasses. Darla had met him on vacation.
She'd left Oregon for her first experience of the South
she loved so much and returned with an Alabaman husband. He had fit into Wilfred surprisingly well, occasionally holding forth about history from a table in the
café. He kept me busy ordering books on philosophy
through interlibrary loans. He also enjoyed detective
novels, which gave us plenty to talk about.

I got straight to the point. "I'm gathering information about the poison-pen letters."

He nodded. He'd been at last night's meeting. "Darla has not been forthcoming about hers, is that it?"

Mom and I took the love seat across from Montgomery. On the coffee table in front of us was a bowl of imitation magnolias and a few copies of *Southern Living*. "Exactly. I wondered what you could tell us?"

Montgomery set his reading glasses on the side table. "I'm not at liberty to reveal what was in the letter. I'm sure you understand."

Of course I did. He wouldn't betray his wife. That didn't mean he wouldn't hint at something that might make her life easier. "What's curious is that Patty told us what was in her letter—she'd burned the original. She's mystified by her sister's response. She thought they'd cleared everything up long ago." I wasn't sure how far to go in talking about Darla's romantic past.

Montgomery seemed unflustered, purposeful, even. "Perhaps new information surfaced."

I glanced at Mom. Could Patty have not revealed all of her letter's contents—or all of the situation so long ago? "I understand that you can't show us the letter, but I wonder if you'd let us see the envelope?"

"You want to make sure it's like the others. It is. However, I'll show you." He hoisted himself from the recliner and disappeared into the rear of the trailer. He returned with two envelopes. "I brought the second one, too. A demand for fifty dollars."

"Fifty? The others asked for twenty."

Montgomery shrugged.

I examined the envelopes. As far as I could tell, they were the same as the others—perhaps even from the same box. They had been addressed in the same hand in block letters. They bore no relation to the one I'd received. I returned it to Montgomery. "Thank you." I scooted to the love seat's edge. "Do you have any thoughts about who is writing these letters? Any idea at all?"

He slipped on his reading glasses again to examine the envelopes. "Someone with deep roots in town. That's all I can say. Someone who goes back long enough to be privy to Wilfred's long-ago secrets."

From Montgomery's side table a book whispered to me. Despite its quieter voice, its words cut through the other literary noise. I recognized it right away. It was the first words of Agatha Christie's *Sad Cypress*, a mystery opening with an anonymous letter. A novel centering on murder.

CHAPTER EIGHTEEN

Back at my apartment above the library, Mom and I pondered the poison-pen situation while I put on the tea kettle. Grandma had always kept a jar of herbal tea, and I'd adopted the ritual, although my lavender and chamomile concoction, unlike Grandma's, wasn't enchanted. The tea tasted like happier times.

"Do you have any—you know—feelings about the letters?" I asked Mom.

Mom quickly switched her focus from me to examining her fingernails. "You know I don't do that."

"Maybe you've had a vision? Something you couldn't ignore?" I pressed.

"You keep asking me that, and my answer hasn't changed." She busied herself spooning herbs into the teapot. "I don't want to go there. Anyway, I'm too distracted right now."

This gave me pause. I hoped her distraction was the situation with my father and not all the time she'd been spending with Emilio Landau.

Before I could probe further, she asked, "That doesn't preclude us from using logic. What do we have for clues?"

"All of the letters appear to be written by the same person. All except mine, that is. Same envelope, same style with cut-out bits from a magazine, and same writing on the envelopes." As I talked, my letter nagged at me. Why wasn't I able to draw anything from it? Normally I could at least get a hit of emotion from anything with words, especially if the words were handwritten.

"Okay. Same writer. We'll come back to your letter later on. What else?"

"They were all posted from Forest Grove," I said. "Lots of Wilfredians go there to get their hair cut or shop for groceries. Things like that," I added for Mom's benefit.

"So it's someone local."

"Must be." This was not a revelation.

"Another thing." Mom rose to take the kettle off the stove. "These secrets are old."

It was true. The latest transgression had taken place more than eight years earlier. "Good point. None of the newer residents—not that there are so many of those—received letters. Plenty of people have let their dogs run loose or turned in library books late since then, but they weren't called out."

"No." Mom was deep in thought. "The question then becomes, why now? If the letter writer has known about these incidents for years, why have they been sitting on them for so long? Why send the letters now?"

I stirred the teapot and filled our cups. Hot tea on a

summer night might sound counterintuitive, but it was refreshing. And calming. I wished Grandma were here now. Maybe she'd have answers. Mom's gaze drifted toward me as if she knew what I was thinking.

"The magic lesson I pulled this week had to do with secrets," I told Mom.

"Really? That's on point."

"Grandma's lessons usually are. I may not always know exactly how they apply to my situation, but they do, one way or another."

Mom leaned forward, interested. Sometimes I forgot that Grandma was her mother and not simply my grandmother and now, after her death, mentor. "I thought the lesson would be about how secrets are bad, how you should always be transparent. But it wasn't just that. Sure, she made a pitch for honesty, but she pointed out that withheld information could do harm in the wrong hands."

Mom stared into her teacup with a wistfulness I wasn't used to seeing in her. "I envy your relationship with my mother."

I was stymied in how to respond. It wasn't often that my mother confessed feelings like this. Even her announcement of her intention to divorce my father was relatively free of emotion. "In what way?"

"You had a bond. She used to take you for walks through the garden and point out the plants and their uses."

I remembered those walks. I was so young that I had to reach up to hold Grandma's hand. She liked to go out in the morning with a mug of tea. She said the garden was more active then, and she pointed to an earth-worm rising from the moist soil, the new shoots of raspberries, or a spider web glistening with dew.

It wasn't plants that drew me, though, but books, and I remembered little of what she'd said, only that magic infused everything we cared about. "I see," was all I could reply to Mom.

"You two share something I never could. The mark."

At the mention, the birthmark on my shoulder warmed. "You're a witch, too," I said. "Maybe not with as much command of magic, but you have the gift. You never talked with Grandma about it?"

Again, gaze to teacup. Then she lifted her head. "She was always preoccupied with someone else, al-ways in the kitchen or garden mixing herbs and casting spells. Someone always needed her. A kid had a cough, a mother needed a job, a neighbor couldn't sleep."

The tone of Mom's voice was a revelation. It had never occurred to me that she might have felt like the one out in the cold. Another thought came into my head. Isn't that what Dad was doing, had done their en-tire marriage? She'd chosen a man obsessed not with magic but with French history. Somehow she'd ex-pected the story to end differently this time. I didn't know what to say—I needed to think this through.

As I pondered, my phone tinged. A text from Toni. I flipped the phone over so Mom couldn't see it.

Mom's expression hardened. She poured tea into our cups. "That's not why we're here, though. The let-ters."

I took her hint that we were finished discussing magic for the moment. It didn't mean we were finished for good. "The second round of letters asks for money. Maybe someone is having money trouble."

"They're hardly asking for much money. Twenty dollars a throw," Mom said.

"The purported sins aren't worth much money. Except for Darla and Patty's letters of betrayal, the worst no-no was fishing without a license. Maybe the letter writer thought they'd stand a better chance of collecting money if they didn't ask for too much."

Whoever had written the letters had underestimated Wilfred's sense of community, even with all the suspicion and uneasiness that had swirled through town this week. I couldn't help but smile thinking of Ruth Littlewood's call to action. The Joint Chiefs of Staff could do worse than enlist her.

"Is there a way to ask around, see what old-timer might need cash?" Mom said.

"Maybe," I replied, thinking of Wilfred's active grapevine. We could likely get secondhand information, at least. It was an avenue of inquiry to pursue.

"What else has changed lately?" Mom tasted her tea. The lavender and chamomile may not have come from Grandma's garden but seemed to hold some kind of magic, anyway.

I set my mug on the table. "Reverend Duffy. People might have confided in him. He'd know about all sorts of goings-on other Wilfredians didn't."

"Josie, he's dead."

I remembered the hot afternoon Mom and I had wandered the estate sale and the stacks of boxes, how his books had grumbled with menace. I sat back. The deck's loose railing and the sharp drop into the canyon.

Lucy's glow, Benjamin's excitement to be home. Adam's hesitation. Did he know something?

"I want to visit the Aerie tomorrow. Adam didn't look great tonight at the café."

"For good reason," Mom pointed out.

"I'll leave him some books and see if I can come away with information about his father. Information that might point us toward the letter writer."

Mom rose and stretched. "Good plan. In the meantime, I'm taking a book to my room. Good night." She kissed my cheek and left, a Louise Penny mystery under one arm.

As soon as she was clear of the door, I flipped over my phone to read Toni's message.

Saw Dad, told him he needs to talk with Mom. He said he can't, he has a paper to give in Philadelphia this weekend. Sorry, J. I tried.

CHAPTER NINETEEN

I rose early the next morning to drive to the Aerie before the library opened. Roz would cover for me, but I hated to take advantage of her goodwill. As much as I loved Roz, I feared her dip into a pessimistic crankiness that would put Eeyore to shame.

Summer mornings in the western Oregon countryside were worthy of sonnets. The pile of books on the passenger seat of my Corolla were especially talkative, although none recited poetry. The book on grief commented in soothing, therapist-worthy tones, and the novels chattered gaily. I'd chosen books for Adam and Lucy that I'd hoped would be helpful and distracting. Grief was cruel. Books were weak comfort, maybe, but the only comfort I had to offer—besides donuts. On the floor was a pink pastry box from the bakery in Gaston.

I shifted down for the climb up the driveway to the Aerie. From here, I couldn't see the deck and its broken railing, but it was in my mind as I parked the car,

scooped the books into my arms—*whee!* they cried—
and knocked on the old Reverend Duffy's door.

Lucy answered. When I'd first seen her, she'd
brimmed with light. Today that light had been all but
snuffed. Every line in her face had deepened and new
ones appeared. Shadows cloaked her eyes. From her
expression, she must have expected to open the door to
a fresh load of sorrow.

"It's you," she said.

"Donuts?" I held the box aloft. To me—to anyone
like me—books would have been the first, best offering. Donuts were a never-fail, though.

Her gaze dropped to the box, already oil-stained and
smelling deliciously yeasty. "Come in," she said in a
weary tone.

I lowered my arm. She wouldn't eat the donuts. She
was probably barely eating as it was. I followed her
into the house's cathedral-ceilinged living room.
Drawn curtains shielded the sliding glass door to the
deck and veiled the light.

Adam arrived from the kitchen holding a mug of
coffee and sat in a narrow chair. Lucy lowered herself
to the couch, and I sat on the stone hearth which made
a cool, if firm, bench. Separated from Adam by a
maple coffee table and lamp was a worn leather recliner with a mandolin leaning against it. The mood
today was light-years from that day only a week ago
when Adam and Benjamin had played together.

I pointed to the recliner. "The reverend's chair?"

Adam nodded. "It didn't seem right to sell it at the
estate sale, but it doesn't seem right to sit in it, either."

"Why?" Lucy said abruptly. "You're sitting in your mother's chair."

I wasn't the only one taken aback by Lucy's tone. Adam's head swiveled toward her. "She died nearly twenty years ago."

"You won't touch her room." Lucy pulled up her legs and directed her attention to me. "They wouldn't even open it up for the sale. No one's been up there for years."

"That's not true." Adam's voice was quiet. His coffee sat untouched on the end table. "I visit it sometimes."

I remembered the stairwell roped off from the sale. At one point, the house would have still smelled of its cedar siding. Adam and Benjamin as boys would have run through it, laughing, while their mother made dinner. Now grief filled the house, and it was souring to rancor. If Emilio Landau bought it, as he threatened, I hoped he'd bulldoze the place to the ground and build something with the potential for calm, if not happiness.

"I wanted to drop off these books, but I admit I had another reason for coming," I said. Adam's attention sharpened, but Lucy looked as if she couldn't care less. "I'm investigating the poison-pen letters." Worried that "investigating" sounded too official, I added, "Ruth Littlewood corralled me into it."

"We didn't receive any," Adam said. "I told you so yesterday."

I glanced at Lucy. Her attention was far away. "I know. Thank you. It's not that. I wondered if your father might have kept some kind of record of his conversations with parishioners. From what I can tell, all the letters referenced old secrets, secrets maybe people confessed to your dad before he retired."

Adam was clearly puzzled. "As in tape recordings? From the church office?"

"Recordings or some sort of log."

Adam was shaking his head before I'd even finished my sentence. "No. Why would he? That would violate every sort of pastor-parishioner confidence."

"He was a strict man," I dared.

"So what? Yes, he had clear ideas of what he expected from the world. From Benjamin and me, too, in fact."

This got Lucy's attention. She lifted her head.

"But keep a log of private conversations?" Adam asked. "For what? Blackmail? He's not even alive. He couldn't have written the letters."

The incredulity in his voice set me aback. He was right, yet where else could the source of the secrets be?

Adam stood, knocking the table next to him. His coffee mug jiggled. "If you don't believe me, come into his office. We kept his personal papers. You'll see. There's nothing there."

"I don't need to—" I started.

"No. I insist."

I didn't want to go into the office again. Despite being the home base of a preacher, something malevolent lived there. The books had leaked energy like poisonous gas.

Lucy's movement on the couch caught my attention. This whole time, she'd been listening but not speaking. The focus in her eyes told me some worrying thought had occurred to her. "Why not look?" she told me. "If anyone in town questions my father-in-law's intentions, you can tell them you checked his office and found nothing."

I caught a hint of a dare in her voice. Her appetite had apparently returned, and she reached for the box of donuts on the coffee table. As she tore into a maple bar, a hand lowered to her belly. She probably hadn't eaten a square meal since Benjamin Duffy died. I hoped Sam was making progress on this case, and that she'd have closure soon.

"Follow me," Adam said.

As much as I didn't want to go into Reverend Duffy's office, I was here, and I saw both Adam's and Lucy's perspectives.

I hesitated, then looped my purse over my shoulder and stood. "I'm right behind you."

Adam clicked the switch on the lamp on Reverend Duffy's desk. "Make yourself at home. We sold my father's books, but you'll find papers in the desk. You're welcome to have a look. Just don't take anything without telling me, okay?" He left.

I stood, alone, next to a heavy wooden desk, in the middle of a small windowless room hemmed in by empty bookcases. What looked to be a stack of church programs sat on a moth-eaten Persian rug next to a cardboard banker's box.

I hadn't expected Adam to abandon me like this. I figured he'd hand me a couple of file folders or, at the

least, watch while I sorted through his father's papers. I
should have been glad to have the chance to peruse
Reverend Duffy's things on my own, without someone
to steer me away from certain desk drawers or without
the uncomfortable feeling of being nosy in another
person's presence. Instead, I was majorly creeped out.

The books were gone, and with them the foreboding
chanting and accusatory hisses, but their miasma clung
to the walls. The skin on the back of my neck prickled
as if someone were watching. No one was. From somewhere in the house—the house that now seemed full of
life and light compared to the study—came the sounds
of running water and the clank of a pan on the stove.

I drew a deep breath and pulled out the chair behind
the desk. Where to start? What was I even looking for,
anyway?

Reverend Duffy's desk was nearly bare, except for
the lamp, a framed photo, and a spiral-bound calendar.
The photo was of a woman dressed for an event—a
wedding?—in a pale green dress with flounces at the
hem. Around her, roses bloomed. This must be the reverend's wife, Adam and Benjamin's mother. How had
she died, anyway? I made a mental note to check later.

Next, I flipped open the calendar's crisp pages and
found notations for doctor's appointments during the
spring, but nothing more. Reverend Duffy had had no
reason to track his appointments lately.

I pulled out the bottom right drawer, the deep one
where files were often kept. Here were more calendars,
going back years. Adam had made it clear I wasn't to
remove anything from the office, so a thorough study

of the calendars was impossible. But flipping through pages from a decade earlier I saw appointments for a number of Wilfredians—some, but not as many as had received letters. Appointments, but no notes. As far as I could tell from the bare office, he hadn't kept notes at all. And why should he?

A drawer on the left held a well-worn Bible. It seemed odd that it had been hidden away. Perhaps the brothers wanted to make sure it didn't get swept into the estate sale.

I returned to the calendars. If I could tie Reverend Duffy's retirement to the dates of the latest transgressions in the poison-pen letters, I'd be getting somewhere. Starting with the latest calendar, I began flipping back, quickly scanning the pages for notations.

"Are you finding anything?" Lucy's voice from the doorway startled me.

Reflexively, I shut the calendar. "No. Nothing definite. Do you know when your father-in-law stopped pastoring?"

Adam appeared behind Lucy. "Nothing in his office, is there?"

Their message was clear. It was time for me to leave. "Nope." I stacked the calendars in the drawer and replaced the latest calendar where I'd found it on the desk. I lifted my purse from its spot hanging on the back of Reverend Duffy's chair and caught a glimpse of white near the wall. Something small. A business card.

Adam and Lucy watched me.

"I dropped my pen," I said, looking away. I was a

lousy liar. I stooped to pick up the business card, pretending I was slipping a pen into my purse.

Only when they'd turned their backs to leave did I dare to look at it. EMILIO LANDAU, it read, with the fanged eel undulating under his name. I flipped over the card. On the back was scrawled *Tuesday, 3 pm*. The afternoon Benjamin had died.

Adam Duffy walked me to my car. I wasn't sure if I should mention it, but curiosity won out. Instead of opening the driver's side door, I turned to him. "My mother's been spending time with Emilio Landau. He says he plans to buy the Aerie. Is that true? Will you be moving?"

He looked away, and morning sun caught the few silver strands threading his hair. "He's said as much, but this is no time to think of selling. Too much has happened."

"I see."

Adam faced me now, his manner collected enough that he managed a faint smile. "Besides, I have a job here. This is the only home I've known."

I took in the Aerie with its modernist angles and raw wood siding. Adam had grown up in this house. Other than a few years to attend college, he'd lived only here in isolated Marlin Hill. His brother had left, his mother died. He and the reverend lived as bachelors up on this hill overlooking miles of quiet forest. Here was his whole life, his history.

"You really think my father could have had anything to do with the anonymous letters?" he asked.

"Honestly, I didn't know. It was a wild card. I couldn't

think of anyone else who might have been privy to so many secrets."

"You might try looking one more place," Adam said. Beyond him, a hawk had caught a current of air and circled the blue summer sky.

"Where is that?"

"The church."

CHAPTER TWENTY

Marlin Hill proper was so diminished that it was hard to picture what it might have been in its heyday. I pulled my Corolla into a rutted patch of road next to what might have once been a corner store. Now it was a home for raccoons and possums, with brush sprouting from its collapsed roof. If the street had ever housed more buildings, they'd been long demolished. The few overgrown driveways extending from Marlin Hill's former main street now led to abandoned houses little better now than moss-laden scrap lumber.

Marlin Hill was a ghost town—except for the church. From the outside, the church was in better condition than even the Aerie. Its whitewashed siding shone in the shade cast by the surrounding forest. As Adam had promised, a key to the church's side door was under the mat, and the door opened easily, as if parishioners poured up its steps every Sunday and weddings still filled it with music. But that was long ago. These days funerals would be its main business. If it had business at all.

The door opened to a spacious office. I flipped the light switches, and nothing happened. The room remained dim. Another door, ajar, connected it to the church's carpeted vestibule. The day outside was warming up to be a scorcher, but here, under the trees, the church was cool. I dropped my purse on a desk and pushed through to see the nave—a grand name for a humble room with a fir-planked floor and barely a dozen pews.

Except for the faint smell of mold and old wood, the congregation might have left the church only yesterday. Hymnals filled the wooden pockets on the backs of the pews, and a red velvet cloth with a gold-stitched cross still hung from the pulpit. I walked toward it, passing through shafts of sunlight crisscrossing the central aisle. A piano stood to the right of the pulpit. It had been freshly dusted. No stained glass, no statuary here. This was a simple church. Simple and sturdy.

But somehow unsettling. The hymnals broke the silence. They began to sing in plaintive tones, each starting a split second after the other, some voices high, others rumbling low. *"A time to weep and a time to laugh, a time to mourn and a time to dance."* My neck prickled. A Bible somewhere announced the chapter and verse from Ecclesiastes.

I hurried back to the office and stood staring at the connecting door. Whatever happiness had existed here had degraded over the years to poison. I let my breathing calm. I was safe. It couldn't touch me. I had come here for a reason. *Focus, Josie.*

The room I stood in held two desks facing each other, but only one looked used. That desk held a desk lamp—as with the overhead light, it didn't illuminate—next to a heavy black Bakelite phone that might have been a sister to those in the library. On a whim, I lifted the phone's receiver. It, too, was dead.

Enough sun filtered through the windows to allow me to see. It danced with shadows from the breeze through fir branches. I picked up a framed photo from the desk showing the reverend from maybe thirty years earlier. His thick black hair was just beginning to recede, but he looked strong. And content. One arm draped over a blond woman's shoulders, his wife and Adam and Benjamin's mother. I recognized her from the photo on the reverend's desk at the Aerie. The upturn of her eyes gave her an air of being ready to laugh. She, in turn, held a toddler against the chest of her gingham dress. A boy, presumably Adam, stood at her feet.

I replaced the photo and pulled open desk drawers to find a collection of pens and notebooks. I leafed through the notebooks. Empty. One drawer held more church bulletins. Nothing much here. Certainly nothing to indicate that the reverend had ever made a record of his parishioners' misdeeds.

I was just about to close the last drawer when a notebook tipped sideways and caught my attention. It was thick and cheaply bound, like a blank ledger of accounts from an office supply store.

I eagerly pulled it out and sat in the reverend's chair.

Could this be it? The ledger's pages were filled with writing, but within seconds I knew the pages held only love. They cooed and breathed gentle sighs. No transgressions here, no recriminations, just happy thoughts.

The faded ink on its pages told me the entries were decades old. I opened it randomly and found a neatly handwritten description of a summer day. *The children are playing tag outside. I hear their voices over the sounds of saws and nail guns up the hill. I hope they'll continue to play on the church grounds even when the house is finished.*

The Aerie must have been under construction. I closed the ledger. Whatever the source of the reverend's turn of mood, it wasn't here. Somehow he'd changed. Had the cause been his wife's death, as Patty and Mrs. Garlington guessed? How this played into Wilfred's current drama, if at all, baffled me.

Still, I was here. Perhaps there were more ledgers somewhere, ledgers keeping a different sort of record. I closed my eyes and leaned back in the chair. "Books, are there more journals here? If so, show me."

I listened. Over a quiet murmur of Bible verses, I caught the drone of the church bulletins reciting programs by day and hour. From a nearby shelf came the unmistakable chant of telephone directories. I focused to make out the tiniest whisper of emotion. I sat up. Yes, there it was. Behind the telephone books.

I pulled the directories from the shelf to reveal two more ledgers similar to the one I'd found in the desk. Making myself comfortable on the floor, I cracked the first one open. Again, happy voices greeted me. To respect Reverend Duffy's privacy, I let my fingers graze the pages to feel their emotion without reading the words. The first ledger gave no hint of the venomous energy of the estate sale books.

At first, the second ledger appeared to carry the same energy as the first—until my fingers brushed the final entry. I yanked my hand from the red-hot page. After a steeling breath, I forced myself to read.

Oh, Candy, my beloved, it read, *what have I done? This I will tell you for certain: It will never happen to anyone else.*

My fingers trembled as I closed the ledger. Something here was very wrong.

I jerked upright to the creak of floorboards. A moment passed, then two, with no further noise. I relaxed. Then a single note sounded from the piano, rippling the silence like a stone in a lake. I froze. Someone was here with me.

As quietly as I could manage, I rose from the chair and crept to the door connecting the office to the church's vestibule. I peeked out. No one was there. Whoever it was was in the church's main hall. I drew a deep breath and marched toward the double doors.

I threw one open and mustered a forceful tone. "Hello?"

Lucy swiveled from the piano bench. With her denim skirt, peasant blouse, and straight black hair parted in the center, she might have been teleported from the 1970s when the Aerie was just a dream and Marlin Hill was a thriving logging town. That vision quickly lifted to reveal the reality of an abandoned, once-loved church

surrounded by buildings the forest slowly but relent-
lessly reclaimed.

Lucy smiled, and I saw a light in her expression I'd
never seen before. "It's you," she said. The smiled dissipated. "I didn't know you were here."

"You didn't see my car?" Why I was wary, I wasn't
sure. Maybe it was the energy of the church that affected me.

"You parked on the street? I walked down from the
other side." When I didn't respond, she added, "I come
here a lot. The Aerie . . ."

"The Aerie has some bad memories, maybe," I said.

"Yes, that's it." She stood and looked around as if for
the first time. "It's such a simple church. Plain windows, schoolhouse lights, pine pews, a wood stove for
heat. Almost Shaker."

"Almost," I agreed. The hymnals were blessedly
silent now. Perhaps they didn't know whose energy to
draw from—Lucy's wistfulness or the poisoned happiness I'd experienced in the office.

"Benjamin told me he used to love to come here as
a kid. He and Adam played hide-and-seek while their
father wrote sermons in the office and did whatever it
is pastors do." She rested a palm on the piano's top. "I
like to imagine him like that. Laughing, young. Before . . ."

I waited for her to complete her thought, but it
didn't happen. "Lucy, has Emilio Landau talked to you
about buying the Aerie?"

My question roused her from some daydream. She
took a moment to respond. "No."

"He wants to live there. Seems determined to move into the Aerie, in fact." Adam hadn't told her. Why not?

Her expression hardened into something I couldn't quite place. Defiance? Satisfaction?

She stepped down to the pews. "That, Josie, is the best news I've heard all day."

CHAPTER TWENTY-ONE

When I returned to the library, a dozen people in Circulation surrounded my mother, as if she were a tour guide at the Louvre explaining the merits of the *Mona Lisa*. Buffy and Thor even lingered at the crowd's edge. I moved closer, and Rodney rubbed against my legs. Could it be? Mom was lecturing them on Madame Récamier—one of Dad's favorite topics.

Normally when my father launched into a mini-lecture on Madame Récamier, about, say, her affair with a French king or the arrangement of her apartments at Versailles, Mom rolled her eyes. True, many of these discussions burbled up when she was in the middle of preparing papers for a real estate deal or elbow-deep in laundry.

Maybe, I hoped, she missed Dad.

"Is that your mom?" Buffy asked, mesmerized.

"That's her," I said.

"Does she boss you around?" Thor asked.

When Mom saw me across the room, she concluded

her talk with, "And, in 1849, she died of cholera at what was then the ripe old age of seventy-one." She made her way to me through her listeners. Buffy and Thor scattered. "Anything new?"

"Follow me to my office." As we left Circulation, I heard two Wilfredians requesting books on the French Revolution.

I closed my office's connecting door to the kitchen and opened the casement window above my desk. It didn't cool the room, but the breeze dispelled some of the stuffiness. Besides that, it gave Rodney a place to perch and watch birds.

"I just got back from Marlin Hill. The timing works out," I said. "I found some of the reverend's old calendars. I didn't have time to look at every entry, but from what I saw, he had appointments with a handful of the Wilfredians who received letters. They were at about the same time as the 'sins' they were accused of. But not enough to account for all the letters, or even most."

"Were you able to get any specific dates?" Mom asked. Rodney jumped to the top of her armchair and head-butted her.

"I didn't even have enough time to photograph the pages. But it looks like Reverend Duffy retired from the church at about the same time as the most recent transgression."

"The stolen eggs," Mom said.

We both shrugged. Mrs. Tohler had admitted to pinching two eggs from the Deevers' henhouse. She said she was baking a birthday cake—the mind boggled to think of how many birthday cakes that woman must bake a year—and the P.O. was closed.

"The reverend had an office in the church, too, so I dropped in."

Mom must have noticed a shift in my expression. "What? You found something?"

I shook my head. "No, but something was off. If you'd been there you might have sensed it." If she'd only open herself to her magic. "Reverend Duffy went through some sort of metamorphosis. Right as the Aerie was being built. The happiness seemed to drain out of him. It's as if he was determined to find doom everywhere."

"His wife died. That would have changed his view of life."

"Maybe. In any case," I reiterated, "the timing works out. But—"

"But he's dead," Mom finished. "It couldn't be him. Unless . . ."

"Unless what?"

Mom leaned back and Rodney dropped to her lap. "Unless he somehow found a way to rig the letters so they'd be mailed after his death."

"What about the demands for money?" I asked.

"Right." Mom stroked Rodney behind the ears. He responded by purring and making biscuits on the chair's arm. "What about his sons? Maybe they over-heard his talks with parishioners and decided to cash in on them."

"Adam? No way. Impossible. Besides, why would he? He doesn't seem to need money, except what it will take to rehab the Aerie. He makes a decent salary and maybe inherited more besides. He and Benjamin."

"Benjamin?" Mom said. "Could he have done it?"

This was interesting. According to Adam, neither he nor Benjamin had received poison-pen letters. At the estate sale, Benjamin had mentioned how grateful he was for the sale's proceeds. Writing poison-pen letters might bring in money, but they were also a sure way to put yourself in harm's way. And Benjamin was murdered.

As usual, Mom seemed to read my mind. "Even if Benjamin were penniless, would he send letters asking for twenty bucks a pop?"

"He'd left Wilfred by the time most of the incidents happened that were in the letters. Besides that, wouldn't he be smart enough to fake a letter to himself? It doesn't add up." I leaned back in my desk chair. "Also, he'd have to have kept a record of what he'd overheard as a child. I don't see it."

"Meaning, if the anonymous letters are connected to Reverend Duffy, he would have had to have written down what people told him, and someone—Benjamin or someone else—stumbled over the list."

At the estate sale, the boxes of books had thundered warnings of evil. Could another ledger have been buried in one of the boxes? Adam and Benjamin surely would have pulled aside anything personal, unless they simply didn't notice it. There was also the problem that I'd found zero evidence that Wilfredians had confessed enough misdeeds to him to fuel the letters. However, it was our only lead.

"Ian Penclosa, the rare books vendor at the This-N-That, bought the reverend's books," I said. "He might be able to tell us if there was anything unusual in them."

"You think he's already sold them?" Mom said. "Unless Ian has been writing the letters, the ledger has moved on."

Ian Penclosa as the poison-pen letter writer. I wasn't ready to believe it—but I wasn't ready to dismiss the thought, either. "There's one way to find out." We had plans that night to have dinner at Sam's. This was my big chance to show him off to my mother. Maybe, though, we could dart down to the trailer park first and see if Ian was home.

A knock on my office door interrupted my thoughts. I opened it to find Lalena, bath basket in hand. Her terrier mutt, Sailor, sat at her feet, tethered by a satin ribbon.

"I know we have a standing weeknight bath date," Lalena said, "but do you mind if I take my bath this afternoon instead? Ian and I have plans tonight." She glowed.

Lalena had a lousy track record with men, but Ian seemed to be changing that. "Okay." Thinking of Sam, I knew how she felt. I couldn't refuse her. "You'll keep it short, won't you? It's our only bathroom for patrons."

"Definitely," she said.

When she left, Sailor trotting after her and Rodney trotting after Sailor, Mom said, "That's the Ian you were just talking about?"

"That's him."

"I guess we'd better try to find him right now. What are you doing for lunch?"

Roz, ensconced next to a stack of books on French history, scowled from the Circulation desk. She flipped open her fan and batted it at her reddening neck and chest. Roz's hot flashes had given her the fan skills of a Spanish dancer.

"You're leaving?" she said. "Again?"

"Not for long," I said, Mom next to me. "Just for lunch."

Roz nodded toward the books and the computer, open to a search on eighteenth-century French history. "Thanks to the interest your mother drummed up, I'm getting to be an expert on the court at Versailles. I'm thinking of setting my next romance there."

I imagined her story's hero, likely Marquis de Lyndon or Viscount Forster, both variations on her husband's name. "Great idea," I said. We left before she could complain further.

Mom slung her purse over her shoulder. "Where are we going?"

"Let's check Ian's trailer first. If his van's there, he's in town and might be home. If not, we'll peek into the café. Last shot is the This-N-That. Maybe Ian will be there arranging his stall."

Summer had made dust of the shoulder of the gravel driveway bisecting the Magnolia Rolling Estates. I was happy to see that Ian had somehow kept Duke's lawn as green and velvety as always. Ian's van was indeed in his driveway. However, no one answered our knock on his door. We tried twice, the aluminum door hot under my knuckles.

"Let's check the diner," I said.

Darla's Café teemed with hungry Wilfredians. The patio was too hot at midday for meals, but inside where the air conditioner hummed, people dug into Sloppy Joes and Darla's signature shrimp and grits.

"Lunch for two?" Darla yelled from the counter.

"Could you make it to go?" I glanced at Mom. Thanks to the witchy DNA that connected us, I didn't need to ask what she wanted. "A tuna melt and a BLT, please. Light on the mayo. We'll be across the street."

At the mention of her sister's antiques mall, Darla turned away. We returned to the hot afternoon and crossed the road to the This-N-That.

The antiques mall was warmer than the diner—fans blew air through the small store, jostling the earrings in Gidget's corner, whooshing the scent of linen and lavender from vintage textiles, and ruffling the ephemera in Ian's stall.

We were in luck. Ian was in his quadrant of the antiques mall packaging up books. He wheeled his chair to face us.

"Don't tell me you're looking for reading material?" he asked. "With a whole library to choose from?"

A set of Dickens novels on the shelf behind him guffawed. I wondered what would happen if I'd brought them to the library where we already had a full complement of Dickens's novels. In the past when I'd had doubles—bestsellers in high demand, for instance—they spent a lot of time bickering and competing for readers.

"We're here to ask about the books you bought at the Aerie," I said. "From Reverend Duffy."

"Those books?" The disappointment on his face was impossible to miss. "What do you want with them?"

I scanned the shelves behind him, but felt none of the doom of the reverend's collection. Chants and spells emanated from some of the volumes, and a book on phrenology lectured about quadrants of the skull, but Reverend Duffy's vibe hadn't lingered. "They might be connected to the poison-pen letters, but I'm not sure."

Ian shook his head. "After a talk with Adam Duffy, I bought the crates sight unseen. I figured, a pastor with a study full of books? There were sure to be some rare volumes, some antiques I might be able to resell, but the haul was a bust."

"In what way?" I asked. Mom had wandered to Babe Hamilton's stall of linens and was examining the trim on a cotton batiste handkerchief.

"Half the books were ruined. Moldy. The other half were fairly common collections of sermons and cheap sets of encyclopedias sold door to door. Nothing I'd want."

"Nothing the reverend might have written in? No ledgers or notebooks?"

"Sorry to disappoint you, but no. Nothing like that. Why?" Ian crossed his arms over his broad chest. "The letters went out after his death, right?"

I nodded. "The offenses in the letters date to when Duffy's church was active and seemed to peter out once he retired. Mom and I had a theory that he might have kept notes of confessions."

"Duffy didn't take confession, did he? I thought he was more of an all-purpose clergyman, not a priest."

"I'm sure he did a fair amount of pastoral counseling," I said.

The books were a dead end. What avenues were left to track down the letters' author?

Mom's voice interrupted my thoughts. "Look at the handwork on these napkins."

I turned to see her examining a fat stack of natural linen napkins with intricately cut and stitched edges. She smiled at Babe Hamilton. I hadn't known Babe was in. My disappointment over not finding the reverend's books dissipated. Finally, Mom would meet Babe, and I was sure they'd get along well.

As I opened my mouth to introduce them, Mom's smile froze.

"May I help you?" Babe asked. Her expression hardened, as well. Both women faced each other like strange cats in a cage.

"You look familiar somehow," Mom said. "I feel I've met you."

Babe backed up a step. She rested a hand on the table's edge and widened her smile. "I don't think so. Perhaps I've seen you at an antiques show?"

Mom shook her head, and her expression softened, like a tight bud relaxing into bloom. "No. No, I must be mistaken. I meet a lot of people in real estate. This wouldn't be the first time I've confused people."

"Believe me," Babe said, "I understand. Same here. Only for me it's the other dealers."

I believed that. For all her sweetness, Babe had a competitive edge. She had to, to get the good stuff at estate sales and auctions. But what was this about Mom's reaction? I couldn't help but remember our discussion about Aunt Beata. I glanced at Babe and searched for a family resemblance. None came.

Mom lifted a stack of pale yellow linen napkins tied in pink grosgrain. "These are lovely. I'd like to buy them."

I returned my attention to Ian. "Thank you for your help."

He shrugged. "Sorry I couldn't do more. Other than the two crates I sold to the Wallingford Guest House, the buy was a bust."

CHAPTER TWENTY-TWO

Wilfred's regeneration had started slowly. First was the retreat center, the shuttle to the airport, and the conversion of the This-N-That. Now came rumors of a new restaurant opening in the boarded-up Empress Theater. The new Wilfred would not be a copy of the old town humming with logging trucks and the rising steam of the mill at the edge of the valley. This Wilfred was firmly in the twenty-first century with a retreat center open to visitors who wished to master everything from Korean cooking to the more arcane points of yoga.

The Wallingford Guest House was part of this growth. I liked watching one of Wilfred's Queen Anne houses transform from an eyesore with boarded windows into the proud home it had used to be.

"This is it?" Mom said when we arrived on the sidewalk fronting the house.

It certainly was. If the gold-edged sign hanging above its entrance didn't inform us, the old-fashioned-style rockers on its wraparound porch and the brand-spanking-new ruffled chintz curtains would. In the market for old-world comfort without actually having to deal with the old world? Welcome to the Wallingford Guest House.

The sign in the front door's window invited us to enter, and we did. Instead of the fragrance of century-old oak that greeted us at the library, here we smelled scrubbed floors and a cinnamon air freshener. Duke must have worked overtime to repair and lacquer the spindled moldings around the entryway. To our right was a drawing room with red velvet upholstered couches and chairs surrounding the shining woodstove. I didn't need to turn left to know it was the library. The murmurs of the books told me.

Janet Wallingford emerged from the kitchen, wiping her hands on a dish towel. "Can I help you? Oh, it's you, Josie."

Ignoring the call of the books, I put on my best smile. "Hi, Janet. I set aside the latest Pioneer Woman cookbook for you." Then, "But that's not why we're here. It's about the poison-pen letters."

"We didn't receive one," Janet Wallingford said promptly.

"Thank goodness," I said.

"What lovely wallpaper," Mom said, gazing toward the slice of dining room that showed through an archway. "Is that by William Morris?"

Janet Wallingford smiled. "Yes, it is. The pomegranate design."

"You must have had a difficult time choosing a pattern. They're all so wonderful."

"I'm still stumped as to which one to use in the newest guest room. We have only two rooms furnished so far. Two more to go," she said. "But that has nothing to do with the letters. Is there anything else you wanted?"

"There is," I said. "It's probably nothing, but I was hoping to look at the books you bought from Ian Penclosa. The books that came from the estate sale at the Aerie."

"Why?" Janet Wallingford asked.

Footsteps skipping down stairs announced Ellie's arrival, her ever-present baton in hand.

"Honey, did you finish your chores?" Janet Wallingford asked.

Ellie studied her fingernails. "Yes."

"No, you didn't," her mother said. "Did you? Show me the work, then you can go out."

Ellie dropped her hands, the baton resting at her side. "Do I have to do it? Now? Why? Famous majorettes don't have to iron tablecloths." She stuck out her lower lip. This might have been cute when she was two years old, but it didn't do her any favors now. "Besides, Mona said I could make a few bucks by taking her foster dog for a walk."

"Ellie, camp is too expensive for us this year. With all this"—she gestured around her—"we can't afford it. Not now. You know that."

"Yes, we can," Ellie said.

My gaze shot to her mother. If I'd talked to Mom that way, I would have been sent straight to my room.

Janet Wallingford folded her arms over her chest. "Go. You will not leave the house until the ironing is finished. It's half an hour's work. You can do it." Then, to us, "I'm sorry. Ellie is at that age."

Ellie Wallingford stomped up the stairs, twirling her baton in anger and narrowly missing the rose-painted porcelain plates adorning the stairwell.

"No apologies necessary," Mom said. "I have three daughters. I know this stage well."

"Could I see the books you bought from Ian?" I said.

Janet Wallingford's shoulders fell. She sighed. "What a waste that was. The books were a good deal, and they would have filled one of the bookcases, but they were in awful shape."

I glanced toward the library. It was cozy, fronting the house, with two armchairs, a desk, and a fireplace. "Not good reading material?"

"No. They were books of old sermons. Packed with rants. And moldy. Half the books had their pages stuck together, and they smelled awful. I had Ellie dump them straight into the garbage out back."

"All of them?" I asked, although it was clear from Janet Wallingford's tone that little had survived. "You didn't happen to notice any logs or journals?"

"There was not much in those crates worth saving," she said. "We might have salvaged a few."

"Do you mind if I take a look?" I asked. "If for no other reason than that I'm a librarian. You know, books."

Mom smiled. "You might show me the William Morris samples while Josie looks at the books. I could give you my two cents. I have an eye for that sort of thing."

Janet Wallingford bit. She led Mom to the rear of the house while I went for the guesthouse's library.

The books called to me to open them, mingle my energy with theirs. I decided on a systematic search. A notebook might be too slender to see right away, and with the chatter of the books surrounding me, I might not hear quiet, methodical entries emitting the energy of only one voice.

The bookcases lining the wall to my right were empty except for a bowl of waxed grapes and a Tiffany-style lamp. The opposite wall's bookcases surrounded a window, and its shelves were half full. I moved toward it and heard one novel shout *Yippee!* Here were a few rows of well-thumbed paperbacks, mostly thrillers and romances. Perfect reads for a relaxing vacation.

"What are you doing?" came a sullen voice behind me.

I turned to find Ellie, baton in one hand and two tablecloths in the other, looking at me. She wadded the tablecloths on the desk.

"Looking at the books. What are you doing?" I asked, knowing the answer.

"The stupid ironing. My parents don't get it." She flipped her baton around her waist and rested it against the desk.

"Parents," I said, as if that could explain it all.

Ellie nodded and poked at the ironing. "I'm going to be famous, you know. I'm practically famous already."

"You don't say?"

"If I wanted to, I could be on TV right now." She refused to look me in the eyes, instead fidgeting with the edge of a tablecloth.

"No kidding?" I remembered Darla's warning about Ellie's propensity for tall tales.

"I get offers all the time. People see my routines and want to book me on their shows."

"I bet." I didn't want to encourage her. "You un-packed the books from the Aerie, didn't you?"

She plopped onto the wooden chair at the desk and faced away from me. "Yeah. Another stupid chore. Those books stank. I tossed them. Mom told me to."

A few of the volumes on the shelves hissed at that remark. I moved around the desk so I could at least see the side of Ellie's face. "What books were there? Do you remember them?"

She stared at her fingernails. "Nothing very excit-ing. I'm sure you have better books at the library. Why?" She lifted her face toward me, one eye shielded by her hair.

"It has to do with the anonymous letters."

She snorted. "A bunch of old people worried about dumb things they did a long time ago."

I sat on the edge of the chair behind me. "You don't like it here very much, do you?"

"Why should I?" She swiveled to face me. "People are mean. The high school coach doesn't know any-thing about baton twirling. That dumb lady who owns the café won't let me show my routines near the patio."

"Do you remember the books? Maybe you kept one or two? I'd love to see them."

Ellie reflexively grabbed her baton and rose. She went around the sofa and tapped a half dozen dark-hued books on the fireplace's mantel. "Those were the only ones that didn't smell like mildew. I don't think anyone will want to read them, though."

Looking at the books, I had to agree. Two were farm manuals that bleated and mooed when I touched their spines. I opened one to faded black-and-white photos of silos. The rest were a variety of Victorian religious treatises hissing warnings. *Attend church twice daily. Cover table legs so not to inspire lust in your neighbor's breast.* I was surprised the book had dared the word "breast."

"You didn't happen to notice any notebooks, did you? Anything Reverend Duffy might have written by hand?"

She looked at me as if I'd sprouted a unicorn's horn and started speaking Esperanto. "No. If you'll excuse me, I have to do my ironing." She pointedly stuffed a tablecloth under an arm.

Something was going on here. Maybe the books hadn't been in such bad shape after all. Could she have sold a few for cash for majorette camp? Or maybe someone stole one from the trash? Anything thrown away would be deep in the landfill by now.

Beware, one of the volumes of sermons intoned, *the devil lurks where you least expect him.*

CHAPTER TWENTY-THREE

I didn't usually have an agenda when I went to Big House. Or, rather, my agenda was simply to spend time with Sam. Over the months our relationship had deepened, and I was coming to understand him. He could have deep focus—when he had a task at hand, the world could explode outside his window and he'd barely seem to register it. At the same time, I was learning that little escaped his attention. He noticed if I changed the part in my hair or hadn't slept well.

Tonight was a different story. Yes, I wanted to see Sam, but I also wanted Mom to see how wonderful it was to have someone to share life with—someone not Emilio Landau. I also wanted Mom to get to know Sam better. I was sure she'd adore him as I did. Finally, I wasn't making much progress with the poison-pen letter situation. Maybe Sam would have ideas of how to further the investigation.

"Shouldn't we bring him flowers? Maybe a bottle of wine?" Mom asked as I bolted the library's side door.

The lowering sun shot golden light through the lawn between the library and Big House. Rodney trotted ahead of us.

The kitchen door at Big House was open with the screen letting in the breeze, and Rodney sat in front of it, waiting.

"Sam?" I said.

He stepped onto the porch and frowned. Happy. To heck with my mother, I moved into his arms for a hello. "Come in," he said. "I thought we'd have gazpacho for dinner. Something cool. I added extra lime—you'll have to tell me what you think."

I glanced back at Mom. Surely she'd see what she was missing? A one-bedroom condo, alone, was nothing compared to this. I knew. I'd been there.

Mom shot me a glance in return. She knew what I was thinking and sent me her own thought, that a one-bedroom condo alone beat a house in the suburbs with a husband who reminded you just how alone you truly were.

"Emilio says your house is a delightful example of 1920s architecture, and he wondered if you have any original furniture and fixtures."

Sam watched us in focus mode, not missing my grimace. "You've been spending quite a bit of time with Emilio Landau."

Mom accepted the glass of wine he offered and took a dainty sip. "He's a fascinating man. Besides, with my background in real estate and his plan to buy the Aerie, we have lots to talk about."

"He's interested in the Aerie, is he?" Sam asked.

Mom was a canny real estate agent, but she specialized in modest homes. She was most psyched when she succeeded in getting a growing family into a ranch-style house with room above the garage for a soon-to-be teenager. As far as I knew, she didn't deal in decrepit pastoral dwellings, even with the *Architectural Digest* lines of the Aerie. I thought of Dad, likely at home in the den with a bowl of cold cereal and a monograph on an obscure Norman monastery.

Sam met my eyes when he handed me a wineglass. He knew something, something about Emilio Landau. Because of Benjamin Duffy's death, he'd be investigating possible suspects. Was there something my mother should know?

"Mom," I couldn't help saying, "we don't even know if Adam and Lucy are selling."

"Emilio can be quite persuasive." She set down her glass and went to the high chair where Nicky decimated some sort of vegetable concoction. She lovingly picked a chunk of carrot from his dark curly hair, then hoisted him from his chair and snuggled him to her chest. It was clear that Sam himself wouldn't be the reason Mom approved of my relationship. "My, my. Isn't he a good boy?"

Nicky let out a joyful shriek, and Mom deposited him on the floor. She smiled as he hurried after Rodney with his short, stout legs.

I smiled, too. If things between Sam and me continued as they were, this life might be mine someday. That is, if Sam could stomach the idea that I was a witch. At least I didn't have to worry about that tonight. This was a future conversation between us. Alone. I looped my arm through my mother's. A conversation I'd like to have, though, while Mom was still in Wilfred. If I had to return home crying, I wanted my mother's shoulder to cry on.

"How's Benjamin Duffy's murder investigation going?" I asked as I took a place at the kitchen table. A platter was already laid out with chopped lettuce, green beans, tomatoes, and more, next to a small pitcher of vinaigrette. "I know you can't tell us everything." Sam and I often discussed his cases, but murder rarely factored into them.

Sam joined us at the table. "There's not much to share. Yet. We're looking at a few angles. Another investigation is chewing up resources."

"But you're sure Benjamin's death was a setup," I said.

"That much is clear. Whoever killed Benjamin Duffy staged it to look like an accident. They wanted it to appear that Duffy had been drinking and stumbled into the deck's railing and fell. A glass and mostly empty bottle of whiskey sat next to one of the chairs on the deck. But no alcohol was in his blood. More than that, the lab says that his body weight alone is unlikely to have broken the railing."

"In other words, he was pushed," Mom said.

"It looks like it."

None of this was new information. "I've seen a stranger around, and he's no yodeler," I said, remembering the man at the diner and library. "There's something suspicious about him. He wanders around town but doesn't seem to have a purpose. Maybe he's from Benjamin's past." Or Emilio's present, I added silently.

"What does he look like?" Sam asked.

"Thin mustache, wiry build, prominent nose. Like a ferret."

Sam leaned back and nodded once. "People are allowed to visit Wilfred, you know. They don't all have to explain themselves."

"What about the whiskey bottle?" I asked. "Any hope of tracing it?"

"The bottle was rare, but apparently the reverend regularly refilled it with garden variety Jack Daniel's. Adam Duffy says the bottle had been in his father's office for years—decades, even. He kept it for special situations with parishioners." Sam shook his head, and a slight smile played on his lips. Something baffled him.

"What is it?" I said.

"Benjamin Duffy's fingerprints were on the bottle. He'd definitely handled it."

"You said the bottle had been in the house for a long time. Perhaps he handled it before he left home. What about the glass he supposedly drank from?" I asked Sam.

"That showed his fingerprints, too. As well as his wife's."

"That doesn't mean much," Mom said. "The murderer might have had something to drink with Benjamin—say, a glass of water—then taken their glass with them and left Benjamin's glass on the table. The murderer then pushes him off the deck and retrieves the whiskey bottle from the office, dumps most of it down the drain, and sets the bottle near the chair, along with the glass Benjamin drank from earlier. All while wearing gloves, of course. A cinch."

Dumbfounded, I looked at my mother. Who knew Mom was a criminal genius?

"The key is to find out who knew the whiskey was in the office and who was near the Aerie at the time of the murder," Mom continued.

Sam nodded, an amused frown on his face. "The answer is that practically everyone knew about the whiskey. Any parishioner who'd visited him might have seen the bottle—or even been offered a shot."

"What about alibis?" I asked. Lucy was not keen on staying in Marlin Hill, although divorce was certainly an easier way out than murder. "For instance, what about Lucy and Adam?"

"They were together for most of the afternoon. Adam had taken Lucy into Forest Grove for a doctor's appointment." Sam knelt to pick up Nicky, who'd wandered back into the kitchen. "That's all I'll say about it, not that I know much. Another team has taken on the homicide investigation while I work on a separate case."

"Emilio wasn't at the Aerie when Benjamin was killed," Mom said promptly.

"How do you know?" I countered. "I found his business card in the reverend's office. Emilio Landau had an appointment to meet with someone at the house the day of Benjamin's death. It might have been with Benjamin himself. Maybe he was scoping possibilities for pushing him off the deck."

"Was Benjamin's name on the card?" Mom asked.

"No," I admitted with reluctance.

"Then the card might have been meant for anyone. Maybe it fell out of Emilio's pocket. Besides that, why wouldn't he meet with the Duffy boys? He wants to re-tire at the Aerie."

Mom wasn't the only sleuth at the table. I forced a smile and turned my attention to Sam. "Maybe the best way to figure out who killed Benjamin Duffy is to de-termine why he was killed. Any leads there?"

I had just finished my sentence when noise on the front porch broke the conversation. Whoever it was had bypassed the doorbell to frantically pound on the door.

Startled, Sam rose. I followed him, and Mom grabbed Nicky.

Standing under the porch light was Lucy, tears stain-ing her cheeks. "Here," she said, pushing a creased envelope into Sam's hands. "I was going through Ben-jamin's things and found this in the back pocket of his jeans. I want it out of the house. You're the sheriff. You take the disgusting thing."

I'd seen enough of these envelopes to identify it at a glance. It was yet another poison-pen letter.

"Open it," Lucy urged. "Read it."

Sam set the letter on the side table and disappeared into the kitchen. He returned with his work satchel and extracted a pair of latex gloves. As he slipped the letter from its envelope, its contents whispered themselves to me. I caught a glimpse of the anonymous letter writer's signature snipped-and-glued-in words.

You think no one saw you. I did. You will pay, it said. Frustratingly vague.

Lucy chewed the cuticle on her thumb and stared at the floor.

"Do you know what this letter refers to?" Sam asked her.

The pain in her eyes yanked at my heart. "Could be anything. Benjamin was no saint, but he'd changed. He really had."

"Did he receive a follow-up letter asking for money?" I said.

Sam glanced at me. I wasn't the one leading the murder investigation. I was, however, charged with getting to the bottom of the poison-pen letters. I flashed him a weak smile.

"Not that I know," Lucy said.

Of course, Benjamin wouldn't have received another letter had the poison-pen letter writer known he'd died. Or had killed him.

Mom and I exchanged looks. What we'd thought was merely rooting out a troubled busybody had just turned into something much more sinister. I may have been charged with finding a murderer.

CHAPTER TWENTY-FOUR

Sam saw Lucy to the door and promised to follow up. Our dinner party was over.

"Sam, what does this mean?" I asked. Benjamin's death linked to the poison-pen letters? Could it be?

Sam stared at the bagged note on the table between us. "I'm not sure, but I'm calling this in."

After brief goodbyes, Mom and I crossed the yard to the library.

We'd barely locked the door behind us when Mom asked, "What do you think?"

An idea about the case was rising in my mind, but I wanted to let it develop a few minutes before springing it on my mother. "Why don't I make some herbal tea?"

Mom dropped her purse on my couch and ratcheted up my living room window to let in the night breeze. A few minutes later, strains of *The Barber of Seville* floated across the lawn. Sam must have already delivered the news about the letter to the sheriff's office and be winding down in his own, favorite way—through music. I nurtured the idea of a ribbon of emotion that connected Big House to my apartment atop the library, a rich pink flow back and forth that only we could feel.

"Tea, yes. And detective work. I know we dismissed it earlier, but could the letters and Benjamin Duffy's death be linked?" Mom said.

The spark in Mom's eyes gladdened me. Except for moments when she spoke of Emilio Landau, Mom's mood had been flat.

I let my hands slide back on the sofa's taut cushion, and my fingers hit a paperback. I pulled it out. "*The Moving Finger*," I said, reading its title.

"The what?"

"*The Moving Finger*. By Agatha Christie, a Miss Marple story. In it the murderer sends out a bunch of poison-pen letters, but they're cover for a planned murder. The killer's goal was to make the murder look like suicide, like the person who'd received the letter was too ashamed to live." I turned the book over, then returned it to its cover image of letters cut from a magazine on a black background. Chilling. "The books put it here for me."

Mom mulled this over. "I see what you mean. The letter writer might have wanted it to appear Benjamin Duffy was so distraught from the anonymous letter that he relapsed, then fell to his death."

"The logic holds," I said. "That, or Benjamin recognized the letter writer and was killed for it."

"Let's be methodical," Mom said. "Let's look first at the letters, then at the murder. Maybe we'll find common ground somewhere."

"Okay." Mom's enthusiasm was encouraging. "There's a notebook on the bookshelf."

Moments later I was seated in the armchair near the fireplace while Mom poured tea. She slid on her reading glasses and lifted the notebook. "Step one, review the facts."

"Fact," I said. "Five days ago, nearly three dozen Wilfredians received poison-pen letters. All of them received a second letter requesting payment to keep the secret, except two: Benjamin Duffy and"—I flinched—"me."

"So far, so good. If the letter writer knew Benjamin had died, they wouldn't have sent another letter." Mom tapped the coffee table with her pen. "Your letter worries me."

"Me, too." I frowned. "Let's come back to that later. For now, we'll concentrate on the others. Second fact, the transgressions in the letters were all committed several years ago and concern people who were in town at that time. Nothing newer than eight years old. Benjamin's letter had to be about something way back. He left town at least a decade ago."

"Yes, yes. We've covered all that."

Rodney hopped on the couch next to Mom and commenced grooming his hind leg.

"In each case except one—the letters to Darla and Patty—the money demanded was only twenty bucks," I said.

"It points to an amateur." Mom made a note. "Either that, or money is not the issue." She set down the pen and looked at me. "Which supports the theory that the letters were merely to lay a confusing background for Benjamin Duffy's 'accident.'"

"Mom, don't get defensive, but I want to bring up another possibility."

"Emilio," she said promptly. She didn't look put out, which was encouraging.

"Yes. He wants the Aerie. Benjamin had made it clear he wouldn't sell his portion, and Lucy, who presumably inherits Benjamin's part of the house, has been equally clear about her desire to get back to New York. She'd sell in a heartbeat. If we're looking for a motive to get Benjamin out of the picture, that's a good one."

"What about Adam?" Mom asked. "Does he want to sell?"

"I don't know." Then another thought occurred to me. If the murderer wanted the Aerie, could Adam's death be next?

"Emilio is not a killer," Mom said. "He's a good businessman. Charming, yes. A murderer, no."

I crossed my arms over my chest in frustration. "What makes you so sure? You've only known him a week. Murderers can be charming, too, you know."

"I feel a sympathy with him. I'd sense it."

Mom's certainty was getting on my nerves. "He wants the Aerie desperately. You have to admit, there's something fishy about it. Why is he in Wilfred, anyway? How did he know the Aerie even existed?"

"It's not a crime to visit the country and fall in love with a charming, offbeat house," Mom replied.

This was going nowhere. If I pressed on, I'd only anger my mother, and I knew better than to tread that path. I took a calming breath. "If Emilio—or anyone else—wanted to buy the Aerie, then Benjamin isn't the only possible victim. Adam has lived there his whole life. I can't imagine him wanting to sell."

Mom was somewhat mollified. "If we assume the letters were cover for murder, then Adam may have received a letter, too."

Adam hadn't been at the meeting in the library's atrium, and he seemed to dismiss the letters as unimportant. Understandable, compared to the death of his brother.

"He said he didn't get one, but I need to talk to him again," I said, "both to be sure and to learn his plans for the Aerie. I should talk with Lucy, too. I can't believe she'd murder her own husband just so she wouldn't have to live here." I shook my head. Lucy had been so distraught when Benjamin had died.

Mom set the notebook on the coffee table. "It's all so jumbled. Yes, we need to talk with Adam and Lucy, but I'm not sure what we'd get out of them."

"We could at least tip off Adam to watch his back."

"Assuming we're right in our other assumptions. That's a lot of guesswork."

Rodney had leapt to my lap, and I absently stroked his silky back. I had something to tell Mom, and I didn't know how she'd take it. "There's one way we could get some clarity, but it would take your participation."

Mom looked at me warily. "What?"

"I wouldn't ask unless I couldn't do it alone." Rodney's purr kicked into high gear. He sensed what was to come.

"Joséphine Ailith, what's on your mind?"

"We could cast a spell."

CHAPTER TWENTY-FIVE

I didn't need to be a witch to see Mom's wariness. She shut down as if a curtain had fallen over her.

"What do you mean?" she asked.

I edged forward in the chair. "We need clarity, right?"

"Yes." Mom stretched out the word.

My birthmark tingled and Rodney's purr continued strong in anticipation of magic. "I haven't yet completely mastered my craft, but I have a lot of power." I gestured around us. "And a lot of book energy to feed into it. You, on the other hand, have the gift of foresight."

Mom's lips formed a firm line.

"With my power and your gift," I continued, "we could cast a spell to give us a clearer view of the letters and murder and any possible link. We might be able to get the perspective we need. A clue or two, maybe an angle we haven't considered."

While I spoke, Mom shook her head. "Honey, I gave that up a long time ago."

"You still get flashes of foresight, don't you?" I knew she did, although she often justified her actions with a simple, "I had a strong hunch." Those "hunches" were her gift. If only she would open up to them. We needed that power now.

"I wouldn't even know where to start," Mom said. "That is, assuming I agreed to this scheme."

"It isn't a scheme. It's a way to bring justice to a situation that has riled up the whole town—and possibly led to someone's death."

The next minute might have been an hour. Sam had shut off his stereo and presumably tucked Nicky in for the night. The room was silent but for the breeze in the oaks outside and Rodney's full-bore purring.

"Tell me more," Mom said.

I let out my breath. "I funnel energy to you. I draw it from the books"—already I could feel the books humming—"and you receive it with an open mind. You let the energy form images or words or knowledge—however you get your hunches."

"Images," she said quickly. "I see things."

I nodded rapidly. "Perfect. That's it. That's all it is. What do you think? We're not harming anyone. We're simply using our gifts to help the town and maybe even prevent another death."

Mom was intrigued, I could see it. She wanted to say yes and she wanted to say no. I was confident I could feed energy to her, but I was less sure of her ability to focus it into clairvoyance.

"Maybe," she said.

One of Grandma's earliest magic lessons had instructed that in magic, yes meant yes; no meant no; and maybe meant no. In magic, you needed to be all in. Mom was not all in, but this was vital. Surely I could convince her.

"First, we form a question and ask it clearly. And specifically. This is the most important part of the spell. Magic is super straightforward."

"What do you mean?"

It felt strange to be instructing my mother after decades of her instructing me in everything from how to tie my shoes to parallel parking to writing a good bread-and-butter letter. "It's like this: Say, for example, that you hate your job."

"I like my job just fine," Mom said.

"I know, but imagine it. Imagine you're sick and tired of your job and you ask magic to fix the situation by saying something like, 'I can't stand this work anymore. Make it stop.' You might think your job will be transformed into something where your coworkers turn from irritating to supportive and you find real meaning. Or maybe you count on a promotion. Instead, magic will take your request literally, and you might find yourself fired."

Mom leaned back. "I see. If we do this"—she caught my eye to let me know she wasn't completely convinced yet—"we'd ask something like, 'Give us information that will lead us to the perpetrator of the poison-pen letters.'"

"That's a start," I said. "But it's too vague. What if magic serves up another murder victim as a way of giving us information? No, we need to be more specific. First, we want the information to come as a vision. To you." I hoped my assumption that we would cast the spell was enough to propel Mom forward.

To my relief, she nodded. "Much better than a dead body."

"Therefore, we need to ask that the information be something we can use to identify the perpetrator before further crimes are committed."

"Do we want a vision pointing to the poison-pen letter writer or the murderer?"

Good question. "After the letter Lucy showed us . . ." I shook my head as if to make the memory disappear. "I can't help but think they're related."

"You said to be specific," Mom pointed out.

"My—our—mission is to find the poison-pen letter writer. The sheriff's department is responsible for tracking down Benjamin Duffy's murderer." I looked at Mom with resolution. "We should focus on the letter writer. If it guides us to the murderer, so be it."

"That makes sense to me, too. Our question might be, 'Show us the poison-pen letter writer.'" She shifted back and forth on the couch, moving her shoulders as she did. Rodney, ever in search of the plushest lap, jumped from my lap to the couch in a single leap. He strolled up to her and plopped next to a hip.

"That's still not specific enough. Magic might give us the vision of a crowd," I said. "We already have a crowd of people to sort through. How about, 'Show us Wilfred's anonymous letter writer in a vision that lets us easily identify them'?"

Mom looked skeptical. "I guess. That still seems to leave a lot of wiggle room. What next?"

Her talk encouraged me. She'd committed. "This next part is at least as important as forming the right intention. You'll need to maintain focus."

"Me?"

I nodded. "I'm by no means perfect, but I've had practice funneling magic to where I need it. You've deliberately shut down your gifts." I hoped my tone didn't sound too judgmental. "You don't meditate, do you?" Even as I said it, I knew it was a ridiculous question.

"I don't have time for that."

"Then we'll have to wing it. We'll ask the question, set our intention, and I'll draw energy from the books. Meanwhile, you'll focus." From the mantel I fetched a brass candlestick with a halfway burned beeswax taper and set it on the coffee table in front of my mother. I lit it. Seeing the flame reminded me of the night earlier this week when the negative force, whatever it was, had tried to suppress my power. Maybe the reverend had been right after all. Maybe evil did lurk here.

Mom watched, curiosity evident in her unwavering attention. "Did my mother teach you all this?"

I didn't miss the slight waver in her voice. "She would have taught you, too, I'm sure."

Mom's gaze dropped to her lap, but her voice was now firm. "That was not to be my way. Besides, I don't have your power. When you were a toddler and your birthmark appeared . . ."

How strange that must have been to mother a girl who had a hundred times your magic—a magic you'd denied in yourself. I rose and kissed Mom's cheek.

Mom drew a deep breath. "We ask, you gin up some magic from the books, I focus, and we see what kind of vision comes up. That's it, right?"

"Yes," I said. "Let me settle down for a moment."

Rodney wasted no time returning to my side. I breathed deeply, letting the warm night air from the open window fill my lungs.

I felt calm, focused. I was ready. I opened an eye to see Mom watching the candle's flame. Good. "Now I'm going to draw energy in to fuel our magic. I'm not sure how much you'll feel." The extent of Mom's power was beyond me. "It shouldn't feel bad, though. To me, it's a sort of buzzing electricity. Sometimes I hear the books talk, too, and lights might flicker. Just relax and let it flow through you. Your skin might warm or arms prickle. Then I'll ask our question."

"Okay," Mom said. From the tone of her voice, I think she was actually enjoying this.

The books were already straining to release their energy. As I opened my mind to them, the power of hundreds of thousands of readers and authors surged through my body in a tsunami-like rush. My body filled up, up, up, and the energy saturated me as if my flesh had become molten lava.

I could open my eyes now, because all I experienced was a miasma of words, scenes, and sounds, from oceans crashing to droll wit to droning lectures. Through the landslide, I sensed Mom and the candle. I could only hope she kept her focus.

"Books," I said. Mom looked up. She couldn't hear the madhouse that surrounded me—only my whispered words. I raised my voice. "Books, funnel your energy to my mother. Enhance her gift of foresight. Allow her to see clearly." Now, what was that question? "Give her a vision of the person behind the poison-pen letters." Our question was something like that. I bit my lip. Hopefully that was specific enough.

I felt the energy swirl and tighten. Now the sounds, smells, and images were so dense they turned white with sheer, glowing edges. They enveloped my mother in a jacket of light. But was she focusing? I couldn't tell. Mom sighed. Her exhale broke the spell, and the light vanished.

And then my living room was as it had always been. The clock on the mantel ticked. The crickets chirped in the night. Rodney stood and arched his back in a stretch before curling up to sleep.

"What did you see?" I asked.

"I can't believe it, but I saw something. For real."

"Tell me," I urged.

"He was looking out a window. It was the strangest thing. Ellie was twirling her baton, and he pulled aside the curtains and looked right at her. He was holding up some kind of document."

"A letter?" I asked. The spell had really worked. Amazing.

"Might have been. I couldn't tell."

"Who was it?"

Mom fidgeted with the hem of her blouse. "There must have been a mistake. Something went haywire."

"No mistake," I said quickly. "I siphoned energy to you and you had a vision. That was the plan. Now, who was it you saw?"

Mom let out a long sigh. "Emilio Landau."

CHAPTER TWENTY-SIX

"We're not going there," Mom said.

"I don't know what you mean," I replied. My brain was already trying to deduce how Emilio had winkled out Wilfred's secrets. Had he snatched something from Reverend Duffy's study during the estate sale? Or filched a book of the reverend's from the Wallingford Guest House's garbage?

"Emilio is innocent. I'm sure of it. He did not write the letters and he certainly didn't murder anyone."

"Why not? Something is off about him—you have to admit that." Mom stared at me, her determination impenetrable. I continued. "He's cagey about his interest in the Aerie. He's seen it, knows how much work it would need, and he knows the Duffy brothers don't intend to sell. Why is he sticking around? It's not like Wilfred is the kind of cosmopolitan center he's used to. He doesn't even like Darla's cooking."

"Just because he refuses to eat cheese before noon—"

"And chicken, never turkey. And only scrambled eggs, also never after noon—"

"Hush, Josie. He has refined tastes, that's all. He likes the charm here. And how remote it feels." Mom crossed her arms over her chest and leaned back. "It's relaxing for him."

"He likes how remote it is, huh? Who wants to be this remote? Someone with secrets, that's who." Arguing with Mom would get me nowhere. I knew that, but felt compelled to continue. "What I don't get is why he would write poison-pen letters." I straightened so suddenly that Rodney leapt from my lap. "Unless he used them as cover to do away with Benjamin Duffy. Lucy has made no secret of the fact that she'd sell the Aerie to the first bidder. All Emilio has to do is bring Adam over to his side." That, or eliminate him completely, was my unsaid addition. Then the Aerie would be his for whatever nefarious purposes he had in mind.

A night breeze rustled the curtains. Stars were thick in the sky, a good thing. A cloudy summer sky meant heat lightning, and heat lightning meant wildfires. Tonight the air smelled fresh, of the Kirby River and fir trees.

"I'm the one who had the vision, remember?" Mom rose. Whatever came out of her mouth next was to be the last word before she stomped to the tower room to sleep. "And I say Emilio is innocent."

I stood, too. "Why did he come up in the vision, then? Why was he waving a letter?"

"I must have been thinking about him. That's all."

The thought of Mom mooning over Emilio Landau nauseated me. I knew it was only a passing crush, a reaction to my father's absent-mindedness, but I didn't want to hear more.

"How about this? How about we clear the other suspects and approach Emilio last? That way if the murderer is someone else, we'll figure it out before we get to a situation that"—I paused to find the right word; I did not want to imply any sort of romantic connection between Mom and Emilio—"troubles you."

Mom couldn't find a way out of my logic, although the way she opened and closed her mouth as her gaze swept the room told me she was trying. Finally, she said, "Fine."

"Good. We'll start tomorrow by talking to Lucy and Adam and see if that leads anywhere. If not . . ." I fixed Mom with a look that finished my thought.

She smiled tightly. "Good night."

Mom was already in my kitchen making coffee when I hoisted myself from bed the next morning. Whispered good mornings from the books wafted up the atrium to me as I passed down the hall, one chanting the title of one of my favorite Golden Age detective novels, *Landscape with Corpse* by Delano Ames. "Hush," I told it.

"What's our plan?" Mom asked as she measured grounds into a cone. She didn't meet my eyes.

"We need to question our top suspects," I said. "Let's try the café, see who's around. Have you had any more visions?"

"No." She busied herself with a coffee mug and refused to look at me. "How do you plan to go about questioning people? We're not the police. We can't compel anyone to talk to us. And they surely won't talk if they have any idea we're feeling them out as murderers."

"Ruth Littlewood set me on this mission, remember? I've been sanctioned."

"Sanctioned to question, not to badger," Mom pointed out. "You've already talked once to everyone who'd received a letter."

This was a problem. I was a librarian, not a homicide detective. However, I also had a burning need for justice, and I had resources no police officer did: I had magic. After all, wasn't finding the murderer now possibly an extension of solving the poison-pen letter issue?

"We need to be subtle about it, that's all. This time we're asking about more than the letters. We need to find out where people were the afternoon Benjamin died. Who was at or near the Aerie? We also need to explore motive. Did any of them have a reason to kill Benjamin?"

"We can't just take their word for it," Mom said. Finally she'd relaxed enough to face me. "We'll need to double-check what they say."

"To the best that we can," I added. "But first we have to get them to talk."

Marching around town demanding answers wasn't going to be an effective way to get the kind of honesty we needed. Sometimes I could use books as an entrée, but none of our suspects had requested anything to read from me.

"Don't worry," Mom said. "This is my specialty. A

good real estate agent can draw people out and win their trust." She pushed the coffee mugs to the back of the counter. "Get dressed. We're going to stake out the café."

We struck gold right away. The café itself was full, but a few people lingered on the patio enjoying the relatively cool morning. One of them was Lucy. She was sitting on the café's patio tucking into an omelet. Tumblers of both tomato and pineapple juice, plus a side of chili, rimmed her platter. It was a lot of food. She must be eating her grief.

"Hi, Lucy," I said.

She managed a wan smile in return. She wasn't as cheerful when I'd seen her yesterday at the church, but at least finding Benjamin's anonymous letter hadn't harpooned her mood even further.

"How are you?" Mom asked with compassion.

She looked up. Dark smudges underlined her eyes. "Not great."

No wonder, I thought, looking at her breakfast. I opened my mouth to speak, but a glance from Mom shut me up.

"Could we sit with you?" Mom asked. "Company is so much nicer on a morning like this."

Lucy smiled grimly but didn't respond. This was enough of an excuse for my mother. She sat, leaving me to pull up a chair from another table.

Darla arrived and handed us menus. "Kind of a small table for you all, isn't it? There's plenty of room out here."

"Thank you, Darla," Mom said. "We'll have coffee with cream. And I'll take the flapjacks."

"Grits for me," I said. There was no way we were going to fit all that food on this table.

"I suppose you're stuck in Wilfred until things are sorted out with your husband." As Mom talked, she eyed Lucy's array of food.

Lucy dropped her fork, loaded with mushrooms and cheese from her omelet. "I want out of this town. As soon as possible."

"Of course you do," Mom said. "This place is as close to nowhere as you can get. Did you know it doesn't even rate being on a map?"

This was not fair. Wilfred was a terrific place to live. Beautiful, friendly—well, mostly—and the library was first-rate. I stifled my instinct to protest, because from the look of Mom's face, she had a plan.

Lucy didn't agree or disagree. She drew a long breath and stabbed at a tomato.

"I need life around me," Mom said. "Nature is wonderful and all, but activity and people are what I crave."

Glancing at my mother, I realized she wasn't simply humoring Lucy. She believed it. All at once, Mom looked younger to me. Younger and more wistful. I wondered what she'd been missing all these years and what role my father might have played in its absence. That said, I was certain Emilio Landau was not part of the solution.

Lucy snorted. The vehemence in her response startled me. "Benjamin wanted to stay. He was sorry he'd left his father and abandoned his brother to take care of him. Plus, he was nostalgic." She shook her head, slowly then faster. "He wouldn't have been happy here. It was guilt, that's all. I knew him. I knew my husband, and he wouldn't have been happy here." Her eyes welled with tears and red blotched her cheeks.

"I see," Mom said.

"He knew he'd let everyone down. He wanted to make amends. He wanted to experience some of what he felt as a boy."

"Tell me more," Mom said.

She set down her fork and leaned forward. "He told us we could live happily at the Aerie. His father had left us enough money to get by for a while. He would start writing music again."

"What about you?" Mom asked. "What would you do?"

"Pancakes." Darla seemingly materialized from nowhere, her arms lined with platters. "And grits. I'll be back with coffee." I had to hold my plate in my lap. Darla, her arms now free, tugged another table to our side. She glanced at Lucy. "More pineapple juice? Maybe a fudge sundae?"

A look of illumination came over my mother. "You were at the doctor's office when Benjamin died."

Lucy lifted her chin. "Yes. Adam drove me."

Satisfied, Mom nodded. At last, I understood, too.

Lucy's voice dropped to a whisper. "Benjamin never knew, never lived to find out he was going to be a father."

CHAPTER TWENTY-SEVEN

While Mom alternately enthused about babies and mourned Lucy's loss, I pondered how I was going to question Adam Duffy about Emilio's interest in the Aerie and to gently warn him to watch his back. I didn't know him well enough to suggest a social call. I'd already shown up at the Aerie unannounced and searched his father's study. Twice would be pushing my luck.

That left one path: my role as a librarian. Adam taught high school music. I had to work today. Could the library produce something in which he'd be interested enough to make a special trip? Or could I call, asking to consult him about our music collection?

I rested my hand on my mother's arm. "Mom, I'm going up to the library to get it ready for the day. I'll see you later."

When I arrived, the library was dark, waiting for people to come and blend their attention with the energy already bubbling from the stacks. I started in the downstairs kitchen, turning on lights and opening curtains. As I walked the ground floor, making special stops to crack the French doors in the parlor and drawing rooms—now Circulation and Popular Fiction—to let in the summer morning's breeze, I could imagine how Old Man Thurston's housemaids must have felt a century ago when the mansion had been a family home and they woke early to open the house and stoke the fires.

I passed through each bedroom, now filled with bookshelves and armchairs with worn chintz cushions, and I formulated my plan. When I reached the upstairs bedroom housing Music, I paused.

"Adam Duffy," I said aloud. I imagined him running his fingers over the bookshelves. "What does he choose?"

The books murmured in reply, some reverberating to faraway timpani, some streaming flute solos, others sounding string quartets. However, none of the books stood out. It was possible Adam used the high school's library for most of his research—or didn't consult much with books at all.

I'd need another plan. What would it be? I pondered this as I unlocked the library's front door and gathered the few books left in the book return.

"Hello, Josie." Patty was standing on the library's porch holding another of the physical fitness books she regularly requested through interlibrary loan. I wouldn't be surprised if she had a box of bonbons at home to pop into her mouth between chapters. "Did you hear Benjamin Duffy's wife is pregnant?"

The lightning speed of Wilfred's grapevine never failed to astonish me. "How do you already know?"

"You were there. Marika Miller was sitting on the café's patio when Lucy ordered breakfast this morning. Marika's suspicions were confirmed when the chili arrived. Then she overheard Lucy telling your mother. From there, it was a quick trip to the P.O. I found out from the cashier when I picked up some cat food."

I held the library's front door open so Patty could pass in front of me. "With that kind of intelligence system, it's surprising we don't know who's writing the poison-pen letters."

"You'll find out soon enough, I expect," Patty replied.

Patty wasn't at the café as she'd normally be this early, before she opened the This-N-That. Clearly, she was avoiding her sister. "I know this is a sensitive topic, but maybe it will help us find the anonymous letter writer. I can't help but think you're not telling me everything about your letter." Patty looked at her feet and remained silent. I forged ahead. "All the other letters"—all except one, that is, mine—"concerned ridiculously minor crimes. I know people got worked up about them, but Darla's and your letters seemed to be the only ones that were serious. Serious enough to split up sisters."

Patty tossed the fitness book on the circulation desk. It wafted 1980s disco and quiet chants of *Feel the burn!*

"I don't know. That's the honest truth. I already told you about my letter. As I said, Darla and I had worked that out decades ago." She shook her head. "I honestly can't say, and Darla won't talk about it. She glares at me and walks away. That's it. We were so close, and now . . ."

Although Darla was normally good-natured, she could be stubborn. Just try suggesting her filé could use a bit more pepper or the grade of coffee might be improved. She would narrow her eyes and turn for the kitchen, leaving the "helpful" customer grateful that Darla hadn't responded.

The answer had to be in Darla's anonymous letter, which she'd refused to show me. In a way, it was encouraging. Whatever it was in the letter that impugned Patty, Darla at least wanted to protect her sister.

"One more thing," I said. "Changing topics. If you wanted to talk with Adam Duffy, what would you do?"

"What do you mean?" Patty said. "You think he has something to do with the letters?"

I could practically see scenarios spinning through her mind and guess how she'd package this nugget for Wilfred's public consumption.

"I'm not sure. We need to eliminate everyone." Not only as poison-pen letter writers, but as murderers.

"You mean, you want a way to talk with him that seems casual, that doesn't let him know he's a suspect?"

"That's about it," I admitted.

"Just call him," she said. "With Adam, you've got to be straightforward. He's had enough students try to play him that he'll find an honest approach refreshing. Tell him you're crossing people off the list, that's all."

I'd already tried this, and after my visit to the Aerie, I wasn't so sure it was the best approach. I also didn't have another ready option. "Maybe you're right."

"Of course I am. And when you do, ask him when Lucy's baby is due."

After Patty left, I stared at the phone. Would Adam be responsive to questions about Emilio Landau's designs on the Aerie? I wasn't as concerned about where he was when his brother was killed. Lucy had confirmed that Adam had taken her to the doctor's office. She hadn't wanted to involve her husband until she knew for sure that she was pregnant, so she'd asked Adam to drive her, with the excuse that they were going for groceries. If Lucy's appointment was longer than an hour, it was possible Adam had time to speed back to the Aerie and kill Benjamin, but Sam would have almost certainly checked this. If he ever got a day off the hot case he was working on, I'd ask him. Would Adam stand for more of my questioning? Before I could second-guess myself, I picked up the phone.

"Adam? It's Josie Way. I'd like to talk with you about the poison-pen letters."

"Again?" He sounded as if I'd interrupted him.

"I have a whole new line of thought. I'd really value your input."

"I don't see how I can help. I've told you everything I know, and you've searched Dad's office, even the one at the church. What more is there?"

"Please," I said. "This could really help."

A moment passed, then two. A library patron paused in the atrium just outside Circulation long enough to stroke Rodney's back then come in. I waved a hand to signal that I'd be with her in a second.

"All right," he said. "I have to come into Wilfred this afternoon anyway to meet with Emilio about the Aerie."

"You're selling?" I said quickly. Maybe I wouldn't have much to talk to him about after all.

"Wouldn't you? My parents died here. My brother was murdered here. I'm getting out."

CHAPTER TWENTY-EIGHT

All morning I glanced up when I heard the library's front door creak on its hinges—I'd have to remind Lyndon to oil them—or heard steps through the atrium. Would Adam actually show up as promised?

Just after lunch he arrived, running his fingers through his hair in distraction. I waved at him and put in a quick call to Roz to cover the front desk. She'd been in the basement embossing covers for paperbacks. She grumbled as she took my place at the much warmer circulation desk and switched on the electric fan.

"Thank you for coming in," I told Adam as I led him toward the atrium. "How about a walk along the river? It's cooler there."

"I'm meeting Emilio in half an hour," he said, but he followed me.

The breeze from the river rustled the dry cottonwood leaves. Their shade probably only lowered the temperature a few degrees, but it was still cooler than the stuffy library.

I plunged in. "I was at Sam's when Lucy brought in Benjamin's letter."

He plucked the T-shirt from his chest to dry it. "I saw it. What does it have to do with anything?"

"It was different from the others." As was mine, but I wouldn't go there. "It didn't lay out his crime."

"I know, I know. It said only that he'd pay." Adam abruptly halted and turned toward me. He squinted against the afternoon sun, which highlighted the tired lines across his forehead. "You don't think that had something to do with his death, do you?"

"I can't help but wonder. Your brother's murderer may have intended his death to look like a reaction to the letter, not just an accident. Maybe they sent the letter as part of the setup."

Comprehension dawned over his features. "Which would mean the letter writer and murderer are one and the same."

"Possibly," I said. "Just an idea."

As quickly as the enlightenment had come, it faded. Adam shook his head. "Then whoever sent the letter didn't know Benjamin very well. My brother was open about his problems with drugs and alcohol. He would have laughed at the letter, not taken to the bottle."

"Could he have had secrets you didn't know about?"

He shrugged. "I suppose so. But how would the letter writer know about them?"

"Benjamin was set on keeping the Aerie, wasn't

he?" I hadn't needed to ask. He'd made his plans clear the day of his father's estate sale.

"Definitely. As I told you, that's not going to happen now. Lucy doesn't want to stay, and the whole place reeks of tragedy. Plus, Emilio Landau . . ." He nodded slowly. We recommenced our walk down the river trail. "I'm starting to get it. You think someone wants the Aerie and killed Benjamin to get it? The letters to everyone—that's part of the ruse?"

"It's a possibility," I said. Rodney appeared from a thicket of blackberry bushes and pranced along with us. That cat had hidey-holes everywhere.

"But . . ."

I knew what he was thinking. I hadn't wanted to consider it, either. "You have to admit, Emilio Landau has been acting strangely. Why is he so set on the Aerie? All appearances are that he has the money to settle anywhere. He looks like he'd be a lot happier in a villa near a five-star restaurant."

"The Aerie is falling apart, but he's offered a lot of money for it."

I'd wondered about that. "More than it's worth?"

"I'm no expert, but my guess is yes."

"I looked him up." At Adam's surprised glance, I added, "He's been paying a lot of attention to my mother."

"What did you find?"

"Not much. A web page for Emilio Landau, but no obvious marketing, no contact info, no social media. His claim to be an art appraiser could be a front." Adam didn't respond, but I sensed he was interested. "What would an art appraiser be doing out here—even one who's retired? Could be a fake name. Let's take it a step further. Assuming Emilio's guilty, why would he want the Aerie badly enough to kill for it?"

"Money. It would have to be that." Adam scrunched his brow. "Do you really think he has a nefarious reason to be here?"

"He might. We can't rule it out, and money is as good a motivator as any." Remembering Emilio's advice on making money to Ellie, Buffy, and Thor, I could see it. Besides, what other motivation could there be? "Then, why the Aerie? What does the Aerie have to recommend it, besides a great view? Is there anything about your house that makes it especially valuable?"

"You mean, like a radium mine or hidden treasure?" He shook his head. "Preposterous. Although . . ."

"Although what?"

"If Landau was up to any funny business at the Aerie no one would know. He wants to turn around the sale quickly."

"He does?" My brain spun. What could he want to hide so desperately that he'd kill for a remote hideaway?

"Yes. Said he'd cut me a check right away if I'd rent him the Aerie until escrow came through. He's serious about living here."

"I don't believe it." If Wilfred was nowhere, Marlin Hill was practically the moon. Try as I might, I could not envision Emilio Landau living in the Aerie.

Adam glanced at his phone. "I'd better turn back.

I'm supposed to meet him at the Wallingford Guest House in a few minutes to talk through details. Whatever his motivation is, I don't care. I'm selling."

My suspicions about Emilio Landau were strong and growing. Sam needed to know. I returned to the library, but I didn't call the sheriff's office right away. Instead, I breezed past Roz at the Circulation desk and countered her protestations with a blithe wave. She was eager to get back to the cool basement and batted her fan furiously at her chest.

I took the former servants' staircase to the top floor. From the habits developed when I lived alone in a big city, I normally kept the door to my apartment locked. The pet door ensured Rodney had no trouble coming and going, although generally he liked being around people and lounged downstairs while I worked. He found great pleasure in lying on the atrium floor, flicking his tail, only to haughtily turn his head away when patrons approached. Today the door was not only unlocked but off its latch.

It was extra warm up here, and opening the windows this late in the day would only turn it into a convection oven. Besides, I was going to the tower room to talk with Mom about the situation and warn her that Emilio was at the top of the list of suspects, no matter what she'd claimed. I gave the door a quick rap to make sure no one was there—the last thing I wanted to encounter was a Mom-Emilio rendezvous—and after no response, I entered.

The room was still and bed neatly made. On the pillow was a note. *J, Out with Emilio. Home for dinner. Mom.*

Couldn't be. I reread the note. Emilio Landau was supposed to be meeting with Adam Duffy. Why would he make last minute plans with my mother? Unless he had to, I realized. Mom might have let something slip about our suspicion of a connection between the anonymous letters and Benjamin's murder. Maybe he decided that silencing her was more important than settling the details of the Aerie's sale.

I let the note fall to her pillow.

Mom was with Emilio—a possible murderer. And I had no idea where.

CHAPTER TWENTY-NINE

I called Sam's work and personal phones and held both of my phones to my ears, ready to speak to the first one answered. Both phones rang once, twice, three times while I paced the few steps up and down my office with Rodney watching from my desk.

Finally, Sam answered the personal phone. "Josie? Is something wrong?"

"It's Emilio. And Mom. He's a murderer, Sam. I don't know where they are." My throat tightened. *Don't cry*, I told myself. "You have to help. Now."

"Start at the beginning," Sam said. He knew me well enough to trust my instincts, even if he didn't know the magic behind them.

I ran through my conversation with Adam Duffy and my deduction that the anonymous letter writer and murderer were one and the same. Who else could it be but Emilio Landau? Emilio Landau desperately wanted the Aerie.

"You say Landau's out with your mother?" Sam asked.

"Yes." I was finding it hard to choke out the words. "I don't know where."

"I've got to go," Sam said. "Don't worry about Landau. We've been keeping an eye on him for another matter, and I doubt he'd turn to writing poison-pen letters."

How about murder? I wanted to ask, but Sam had hung up.

I stared at the phone. Sam had said they were watching Emilio Landau. Why? Sam and the crew at the sheriff's office were capable professionals, but I couldn't sit around while my mother's life was in peril.

As I dashed out of my office, through the kitchen, I heard Roz yelling at me to come back. I ignored her and ran up the drive, over the Kirby River, and down the hill, gasping to keep my breath. Babe Hamilton waved from the entrance to the This-N-That, but I couldn't stop long enough to do more than nod. I slowed my pace to a brisk walk and calmed my breathing as I approached the café. A minute later, I left. Neither my mother nor Emilio were there. Where could they be?

I crossed the road and plunged into Wilfred's small residential neighborhood. The houses—a collection of Victorian shotgun shacks and ranch homes with a few larger farmhouses interspersed—dozed in the afternoon heat with blinds drawn against the sun. In contrast, the Wallingford Guest House loomed cool and welcoming on its shaded corner lot.

And it was not dozing one bit. Two sheriff's cruisers were parked out front. Already. I'd called Sam less than five minutes earlier. He wasn't kidding when he said they'd been keeping an eye on Emilio.

I hurried up the porch steps, and a deputy at the front door stopped me. "No one's allowed in. Police business."

I peered behind him but couldn't make out anything but an empty foyer and darkened hall to the kitchen. The party must be upstairs. "Is my mother in there? Nora Way?"

"No one is allowed in," he repeated.

"I just want to know if my mother is all right," I said. The deputy shook his head. I couldn't feel Mom's energy, but it might be obscured by other hot emotions.

"They're not going to let you in," a girl's voice said.

I turned to see Ellie Wallingford rocking on the porch swing, dangling her baton. The sheriff's deputy closed the door to keep his post in the air-conditioned interior.

"What's going on in there?" I asked.

"I didn't see your mom." Ellie tossed the baton without looking at it, and it twirled gracefully before landing gently in her palm. "They came like ten minutes ago to talk with Emilio."

Emilio Landau was here. I sat on the porch railing near Ellie. Heat had brought out the sweet scent of the baskets of petunias hanging from its ceiling. "Do you know why?"

She shrugged and her baton flipped across her shoulders to her other hand. "They're looking for something. They think Emilio has it."

My mother was not here. My shoulders sagged in relief. My level of tension dropped a few notches, but not completely. Too much was unknown.

Ellie fixed me with her gaze. "You're trying to figure out who wrote the letters, aren't you?"

"Uh-huh." Emilio Landau had a clear motive for Benjamin's murder. I tapped at the porch railing. He wanted an out-of-the-way headquarters for some nefarious activity, and the Aerie fit. Benjamin refused to sell, so he eliminated that obstacle. He somehow gleaned information about Wilfredians from the estate sale then used it to fake Benjamin's relapse and fatal accident.

But what about Emilio's alibi? He'd been with my mother the afternoon Benjamin was killed. Mom wouldn't lie. There was no way he could have pushed Benjamin off the deck. I remembered the rat-faced stranger taking coffee at Darla's and loitering at the library. Could Emilio have had an associate kill him?

"I bet you'll never figure it out." Ellie asked. "The letter writer has been extra crafty."

"I wouldn't be so sure. My thought is that the same person who wrote the letters killed Benjamin Duffy." I chided myself for letting a thirteen-year-old girl get my back up.

Ellie's baton hit the porch with a clatter. "You've got to be kidding."

"Why not? The letters might have been a front. Benjamin's letter was really vague. Maybe the letter writer wanted people to think he relapsed or jumped off the deck himself when he saw it."

"Benjamin's letter?" Ellie said, her voice rising.

I nodded. "He got one, too. Lucy brought it in. She said Adam found it. Maybe the sheriff's office figured out that Emilio is the culprit."

Ellie jolted to her feet and ran for the front door, but the deputy wouldn't let her in. "Emilio!" she yelled past him. "Let me in. You're making a huge mistake. He's not a murderer!"

My mother was clearly not the only female who had fallen for Emilio's charms. If only I knew what was happening upstairs. Rodney, seeming to appear from nowhere as usual, head-butted my calf. I looked down into his citrine-tinted eyes, and a plan materialized.

"Ellie, are you thirsty?"

She dropped her arm to her side, her baton clicking on the porch floor, and looked at me like I'd lost my mind. "What?"

"It's warm on the porch. I was thinking we could use something to drink while we wait to see what's happening in there."

"Why are you here, anyway? I told you your mom isn't inside." Ellie tapped her baton on the porch railing. "They're a bunch of screwups, anyway. They've got it all wrong."

We'd see about that. I reached into my purse and pulled out a ten-dollar bill. "How about if you run down to the P.O. Market and get us a couple of iced teas? Plus whatever else you want. I'll wait in the backyard."

Ellie hesitated only a moment before snatching the bill. "Okay. But don't let the police leave until I've talked to them."

As she hurried down the street, I circled the house to

the backyard and settled into a chaise longue in the shade of an oak tree. Rodney jumped into my lap. "You know what we're going to do," I told him. "I'm not sure what we're looking for, but we need to be thorough. And keep our ears open. Got it?"

With that, I placed my hand on his head and stared into his eyes. *Focus.* In a moment, I was looking at myself, drowsy and half-conscious. The world had flattened—things close to me were fuzzy, but the motion of every bird, every flying insect plucked at my attention like harp strings.

Go, I urged Rodney. *Inside.*

Rodney leapt to the grass and trotted around the front of the house. Through his eyes I was close to the ground with the scent of fresh earth in my nostrils. Rodney paused at a crack in the siding circling the porch. He smelled a mouse.

No. Not now, I willed him. *We have a job to do.*

Rodney reluctantly pulled away and darted up the porch stairs. Without looking up, he dashed past the deputy on guard.

"Hey," the deputy said. "Shoo!"

Rodney—with me as his mental passenger—ran up the carpeted stairs. He paused on the landing. Straight ahead was a bureau with a dust bunny under it. To the left were two closed doors, likely guest rooms. Conversation came through the transom of a room on the right.

Rodney nudged the door. It opened, and he slipped in. *Under the bed*, I whispered.

Rodney easily slipped under the high bed. From here, we saw two sets of feet: Sam's, in his work boots, at a chair at a desk set in the bay window. Directly in front of us were polished loafers and black silk socks on what could only be Emilio's feet.

Ellie had been right—my mother was not here.

"You don't deny that Emilio isn't your birth name," Sam said. He sneezed. Cat allergy. Rodney backed up a few inches.

"No. Why should I deny it? 'Roger' hampered me in my profession." His voice was calm, even amused. "Emilio suits me better. I don't know why it should concern you."

"And the accent?"

"Again, the vocal cadences of New Jersey don't tantalize art buyers like a continental turn of phrase does."

Rodney was too far under the bed to see Sam's expression, but I sensed a tight smile. He was frustrated. "You know what we're looking for," Sam said.

"Yet you have no search warrant. Sheriff Wilfred, I begin to feel insulted. Should I contact my attorney?"

Sam's phone chimed. Leather slithered as he slipped the phone from his belt. A pause. Rodney jumped back as the desk chair scooted on the wooden floorboards. Sam stood. "I'll be back in a moment with that search warrant. And, yes, you have a right to legal representation."

Rodney and I turned to watch Sam's boots cross the floor and leave the bedroom.

The second Sam's footsteps sounded on the landing, Emilio sprang to his feet and crossed to the closet. He withdrew a suitcase and rested it on the bed above us. Clicks told us he'd opened it.

Seconds later, Emilio's loafers crossed to the bay

window. Rodney inched from under the bed to see more clearly what he was doing. Emilio reached over the desk, lifted the window, and dropped something. Just as quickly, he shut the window and returned the shades to their half-closed position. Rodney backed under the bed just as Emilio closed the suitcase and returned it to the closet.

At a rap on the door, the mattress squeaked above us. Emilio sat as if he'd never left.

Sam entered with two deputies. "Everything is in order."

Emilio apparently looked at something Sam tendered, because he replied, "I see. Well, gentlemen, have at it. Should I remain here or wait downstairs?"

"There's a cat under the bed." Rodney—along with me—turned to see a face wearing a pair of glasses and the gloved hands of someone reaching toward us.

At the same time, in the garden someone shook my shoulders. "Josie, wake up."

I was back in the chaise longue. "Sorry. It was so warm out here, I guess I dozed off."

"I got you a seltzer water." The cheapest thing in the store. "I'm having soda and a box of Ding Dongs. There are more sheriffs here."

I barely heard her. Emilio's room was directly above me on the second floor. Below his window was a hedge of roses. And peeking from their base was a brown cardboard tube.

I gingerly reached around a bush heavy with white roses and eased the tube from the shrubbery. In the afternoon heat, the streets were quiet. Even the birdbath was still as finches stayed in their nests waiting for the cooler evening. I uncapped the tube and pulled its contents, a roll of canvas, from its interior. I smoothed it open.

It was a painting, only as large as a notebook. But, oh, what a lovely painting. On it, a cool river flowed through a misty twilight of an impossible but dreamy blue-green-gray with clouds of oak trees along its banks. In the lower righthand corner it was signed. Pierre Bonnard.

CHAPTER THIRTY

That evening, Wilfred practically vibrated with the news of Emilio Landau's arrest. A high-end art trafficker had been in our midst. It was almost as exciting as when the Donaldsons' pig got loose and chased Mrs. Garlington's now-deceased beagle through town. The foray had ended in a partnership between the animals, resulting in both of them darting into open houses and stealing dinners in the making. At one house, the beagle had made off with an entire pot roast.

Tonight, all around town, people sat on porches or on the café's patio as the day cooled, and they talked. I'd been worried about how Mom would take the news, but she was bizarrely calm—satisfied, even. We'd returned to the library after a slice of Darla's peach pie, and, at last, I had the chance to talk with her alone.

"You seem okay," I said as we approached the library.

She looked at me, and understanding flowed between us. Having a mother with magic in her blood was an advantage at times. "It was nice to have Emilio's attention," she said. "And it's nicer now that I don't have to figure out how to let him down."

I halted in the garden between the library and Big House. "You never seriously considered starting something with him, did you?"

"No. Not really."

I didn't like the sound of this at all. "Casually, then?"

"Spending time with Emilio was a way to look at your father in a different light." She smoothed a gray curl behind an ear. "I'm not even sure Emilio plays on our team, if you get my drift."

"You compared Emilio Landau to Dad?" My voice might have hit a higher pitch than necessary. "I can't believe you'd even—"

"I don't expect you to understand, Josie. Your father and I have been married thirty-five years. He doesn't see me anymore, and, to be fair, maybe I don't see him. Emilio was charming. He noticed things about me. I never seriously entertained the thought of running off with him. I just wanted to know what it would feel like to have a man's attention again." She shrugged. "Of course, he was a felon, but you can't have everything." Mom nodded at the window facing Big House. "Look. Sam's pulling up."

The sheriff's department SUV crunched gravel behind us. Sam rolled down his window. "Josie, Nora. I was planning to call. Would you like to have dinner with me tonight?"

I needed a spot of normalcy in my life right now.

Dinner with Sam would fit the bill perfectly. His company would soothe the drama kicked up from Benjamin's murder, Mom and Dad's relationship issues, and the poison-pen letters. Besides, Sam would have the inside scoop on Emilio Landau.

"I'd love that. Truly," I said.

Mom looked first at Sam, then at me. "You go ahead, Josie. I'd like a quiet evening alone."

As much as I loved my mother, my heart leapt. Sam. All to myself. "Thank you, Mama." I hadn't called her that in years. I kissed her cheek. "I love you."

Half an hour later I was standing next to Sam and slicing basil into julienned strips while a breeze blew through the kitchen's screen door. Bliss.

"So," I ventured, "Emilio Landau."

Frowning, Sam laughed. "I was wondering when you'd ask."

I moved sideways to bump my shoulder with his. Once again I silently thanked the fates that had brought us together.

"The feds have been after Landau for a long time and traced him here. You know the man you saw last week at the café?"

"The ferret-looking guy? He was a federal agent?" I shook my head. "I saw him at the library, too. Even with the alpine hat with the feather stuck in it, I knew he wasn't from the yodeling workshop."

"Interpol. They traced Landau from Bruges to

Philadelphia, then to Portland and finally to Wilfred. My old boss at the FBI knew I was here and put me on the spot to follow up."

I set down the chef's knife and took a seat at the long kitchen table. "Why Wilfred?"

"He was after the Aerie in Marlin Hill. Wilfred is obscure enough, but Marlin Hill teeters on the edge of not existing at all. It's the perfect place to hide stolen art."

"How did Emilio even know about Marlin Hill?" I asked.

"It's interesting," Sam said. "His father was the architect who built the Aerie. He moved his family here during construction. Emilio, an adult by then, was his assistant, and he never forgot Marlin Hill."

"Patty mentioned that he looked familiar, but she shrugged it off." So had I. I imagined Wilfred and Marlin Hill in the 1980s when steam churned from the timber mills and the towns were vibrant and busy. "How was Emilio planning to use the Aerie?"

"As a cooling-off area. Art thieves would steal paintings or sculpture or whatever, mostly from private homes and corporate collections, and smuggle them to Portland."

"By plane?"

"Sometimes, but mostly by cargo ship. That way the goods would be more likely to fly under the radar. A painting hidden among containers of frozen tuna was easier to pass through." Rodney jumped to my lap and dipped his head under my palm. He smelled of the rosemary bush Lyndon kept near his cottage. "Then

Landau planned to transport the art to the Aerie and let it sit a while. Years, if need be. I wouldn't be surprised if he aimed to convert the church into a storage area by fitting it with climate control."

"He could keep the outside looking abandoned, but the inside would be high tech."

"Correct." Sam took the seat next to mine and rested his hand on my shoulder. "Right now, this is all conjecture. We're still figuring things out. One thing we know for sure, though, is that he's the man we've been looking for." His thumb swept my collarbone. "Thanks to the Bonnard you found."

I smiled. It had been a glorious moment, calling the sheriff's office back to the guesthouse to show them the evidence. I'd had the honor of handing the painting to the very deputy who'd refused me entry earlier. The only black spot was Ellie Wallingford's wailing. She'd waved her baton and shouted about Landau and murder and a lot of incomprehensible things. It had only ended when her mother had sent her to her room and grounded her for the night.

"How badly did Emilio Landau want the Aerie?" I asked.

"Do you mean, did he want it badly enough to kill Benjamin Duffy?"

I nodded. "You'd be a hero, rounding up both an art fence and a murderer."

"He doesn't have a record of violent crime and his alibi holds. I'm afraid Benjamin's killer is still out there. Speaking of, how did Nora take the news about Landau?" Sam asked.

He was so considerate, my crazy and wonderful man. He would never take me for granted as my mother claimed my father did. Or was I too smug? Both men had had knuckle-down focus when they were on a trail. "Surprisingly well. She was almost philosophical about it. She might be talking to Dad right now." I was more hopeful than convinced.

Sam rose to carry on with dinner prep, a risotto full of summer vegetables. "Did your parents have a troubled marriage?"

"No. I mean, not that I could see. They seemed to coexist happily." Maybe that was the problem, I thought. They coexisted, not meshed. Dad had his studies to distract him, and Mom hid her witch bloodline to the point of denying my sisters' and my magic. "I realize now that my mother never shared an important part of who she is with my father."

Sam turned to me. He wouldn't ask me what that was—he was too respectful. But he wanted to know, and I needed to tell him. My secret agitated me like a boil that demanded to be lanced. I wouldn't let happen to us what my mother let happen to my parents' marriage. Sam had to know I was a witch, even if it meant he would leave me. He had to know.

"I'm sorry about that," Sam said. "As I learned the hard way through my marriage to Fiona, honesty is essential to a good relationship."

A fire lit in my chest—the heat of fear, not love. What I was about to say could ruin us for good. I drew breath deep into my chest. "My mother . . ."

Sam watched me with compassion. "You don't have to tell me if it makes you uncomfortable."

"I need to tell you." It wasn't only because of the letter. It was the right thing to do. Besides, if things went south, at least I could cry in Mom's arms. I closed my eyes. *Do it.* "My mother is a witch." I opened my eyes to a look of puzzlement on Sam's face.

Then he frowned. Amused. "A few days ago you said something like that about yourself. You've certainly cast a spell over me."

"Seriously, Sam. It's in my family. All the women are witches. I'm an especially powerful one." It was easier to talk, now that I'd started. When Sam didn't reply, I continued. "You know that birthmark on my shoulder?" He knew it. He'd touched it and even kissed it. "It marks me as having unusual magic. My grandmother had one, too."

His frown faltered. "This is a joke, right? A play on women's intuition?"

"The magic my mother and sisters have is something like intuition, but stronger. Everyone has a smattering of that kind of magic. You know how sometimes when you answer the phone you already know who's calling?"

"There's caller ID."

"I mean when your phone's on the table and you can't see it. Here's another example. Have you ever met someone and had the feeling you've known them before, even though it's impossible?"

He pushed one of my curls behind an ear. "I do know that feeling. I felt it when I first saw you."

I let my mind wander for a moment to that night, one of my first in my apartment above the library, when I found Sam downstairs, asleep with a Hardy Boys mystery open in his lap. I'd felt it, too. Finding him was like uncovering a limb I'd never known was missing. "That phenomenon is magic. I have it in spades."

Sam watched me with a half smile. Perhaps he wondered if I was joking, but my serious expression surely told him otherwise. Maybe he suspected the stress of the past days had strained my mind to lunacy. Whatever he thought, he certainly wasn't considering the possibility that I was a bona fide witch.

"I know it's a lot to take in," I said.

He withdrew his hand from my arm and examined me. "I'm not sure what you're trying to tell me."

He needed proof. He needed evidence he could understand, but I feared it was only going to bewilder him further. "It's like this: I can transform energy into knowledge and action." I looked up. Sam's gaze had taken on the focus he showed when he was at work. "I don't profess to be an expert in witchcraft. I only know what I've learned over the past few years." No sense getting into my grandmother's letters now. "Different witches have different sources of energy. Mine comes from books."

His intense gaze was inscrutable. Did he believe me, or did he think I'd gone off my nut? "This is a joke, right? You're pulling my leg."

A crow cawed outside the window. It scratched on the windowpane. We watched it fly off.

My throat tightened. "This isn't easy for me, Sam. I know it's hard to understand. There was a time when I would have laughed it off, too. But it's real. I'm a witch. I can do things the average person can't."

He drew a finger down my bare arm, then let his hand fall to his side. "Prove it," he murmured.

"Okay." This would be the only way he'd believe me. A bookshelf in the living room held a set of encyclopedias and a varied collection of novels. Merely sensing I was thinking of them, the books began to chatter. "Go to the living room and pull a book off the shelf. I'll stay here and tell you what it is."

Sam disappeared through the arch to the dining room. I leaned back. I might not get dinner tonight, whether I made him a believer in magic or not. This was a lot for the average man to take in.

"Got it," he said.

"*The Mysterious Miss Morissot*, by Valentine Williams." A mystery from 1930, the novel informed me, set in France. I centered my mind, bringing my focus away from the worry swirling in my chest. "Now let the book fall open and place your finger somewhere randomly on the page."

"Done," Sam said.

"You're on page forty-six, chapter eight, am I right?" I cleared my throat and recited the words as they unspooled in my mind. " 'Oliver Royce ran down the beach, shed dressing gown and slippers on the edge of the idly lapping waves, and plunged into the sea. It was a mother-of-pearl morning.' "

Sam didn't reply. A moment later he was in the kitchen. He set the book on the table so its title faced me, and leaned against the wall, his arms folded over his chest. "I don't know what sort of parlor trick this is, but I can't wait until you explain it to me."

"It's for real," I whispered. My emotions flashed hot, and combined with the magic I'd just summoned, the house's electric lights flashed and crackled. The book on the table turned 180 degrees and now faced Sam. Did I really want to do this? I had to. I looked Sam in the eyes. "Watch."

Now I closed my eyes and felt magic tighten inside me like a funnel cloud. Sam's grandmother had been a reader—the novel had been hers—and the various books throughout the house had been waiting decades to release their energy.

"Books," I said. "Come to me."

Sam raised an eyebrow. *The Mysterious Miss Morissot* snapped to attention and slid to the table's corner. Sam's arms dropped to his sides. One by one, slowly at first and then quickly, books sailed into the kitchen at shoulder height and clunked to the table, arranging themselves by size so they constructed a tight layer, creating a plane of novels, cookbooks, biographies, children's picture books. A second layer built itself over that one, then a third. The books kept coming. Sam's jaw had tightened.

"Make it stop," he whispered.

"Stop," I said, and the funnel of energy dissipated. The books in midair dropped to the ground with thuds throughout the house.

Sam simply stared.

I faced him full-on. "This is who I am." I stepped forward to kiss him, then thought better of it. He needed time to absorb what he'd just experienced. I understood—it had taken me a long time to accept it myself. I stepped to the kitchen's screen door and rested a hand on the doorknob.

Silent, Sam watched me.

Reluctantly I stepped outside. "I'll be in touch."

CHAPTER THIRTY-ONE

"I told him," I said to Mom.

My mother looked up from her phone where she was completing the daily word puzzle and, if I was right, trying to distract herself from her own drama. She shifted on my sofa to get a better view of me. "Are you sure he understood? He didn't take 'witch' in the sense so many men do—you know, 'witchy woman' and things like that?"

I took the armchair near the fireplace. "Nope. He knows. I used my magic to move books. He saw it firsthand."

Mom set her phone face down on the coffee table. "How do you feel?"

No matter how old you get, sometimes nothing will do but a mother's sympathy. Emotion welled within me. "Mom," was all I could say.

She patted the cushion next to her on the sofa, and I took the spot and leaned into her faint fragrance of lily of the valley. "I'm in shock, I guess. I think Sam is, too. I don't know what to think or say."

Mom smoothed my hair—or tried to, anyway. The curls made it difficult. "Sam is a good man. Once he gets used to the idea, he'll be okay."

I lifted my head. "Is this something you know? As in, *know* know?"

She sighed. "It's a mother's intuition, not a vision. But even if I'm wrong, this was still something you had to do."

"You're right." I let my gaze drift toward the window, knowing Sam was out there, across the garden. Tonight, he might lie awake in his bed, replaying the evening in his mind. Above, stars were thick in the summer sky, as deep and full as cream, rich with shooting stars.

"I should have known you were using magic," Mom said.

"Why is that?"

"I could feel the restless energy."

I raised my head. "All the way here?" From Sam's, I hadn't been able to draw energy from the library's books. Besides, I hadn't needed to. Perhaps my magic had reach I didn't even know.

Mom's brows drew together. "It didn't feel altogether . . . right."

I twisted to face her. "What do you mean?"

"It's that sensation, the one I've been getting hits of off and on the whole time I've been in Wilfred. I thought it was because of the situation between your father and me, but I'm starting to think something else is at play. Something more ominous."

My neck prickled. There it was again, the suspicion that a force of magic—not my magic—was at work. But, why? Why would dark magic track me here? And who was at its center? "Maybe it will go away."

"I don't know," Mom said.

"Maybe we're confusing emotional and magical energy."

She dipped her chin and looked at me. "There's overlap for sure, but something else is happening here. Don't you feel it?"

I nodded slowly. "When you met Babe Hamilton, I thought you had some kind of reaction. Do you—?"

At that moment, a crystal vase tumbled from the end table and shattered, spilling water and dahlias. Both Mom and I leapt to our feet. Mom gasped. I stood, my hand flat on my chest.

"I swear that table is solid," I said.

We stared at the wreckage. What was going on? It was minor energy, however. Just an annoyance. Malevolent, maybe, but it didn't compare to the force of my own magic—at least, I hoped not.

"Babe Hamilton?" Mom said, drawing out each syllable.

"At the This-N-That." My pulse slowed.

"I don't recall her."

"The booth where you bought the napkins. You remember."

"Oh, yes. The napkins. They are lovely."

I waited for Mom to say more, but she didn't. "I

can't worry about it too much. I'm curious, yes. Panicked, no." There was too much else going on to freak out about a drift of disturbing energy.

"Don't be so hasty, Josie. This magic has been persistent. It troubles me." Mom was already headed for a broom and dustpan. "And you've always been a big one for denial."

"Ha ha." I used the moment Mom was fetching cleanup materials to catch my breath. "How do you feel about the situation with Emilio? Still okay?"

I was relieved to see Mom's expression unchanged when she returned. "Easy come, easy go. Honestly, it was just nice to have the attention, feel appreciated again as a woman. I'm not surprised he was dealing outside of the law."

"Really?" I threw a towel over the spilled water, now that the vase had been swept up.

Mom's gaze drifted to a corner of the room. "He's so picky about food. Much more than a normal man. That would have driven me nuts. Gerard appreciates everything I put on the table for him. His attention might wander, but he never fails to notice new recipes, especially variations on French favorites. I saw a vegetarian cassoulet he might like."

"You're thinking of going back to Dad?" I said quickly.

"I didn't say that." Mom shuffled a bit on her cushion. "I just pointed out that not everything about your father is objectionable."

Maybe Mom had the gift of foresight—or would, if she chose to set it free—but I had the understanding of a daughter who had seen both parents through more than three decades. I wasn't going to let their marriage disintegrate so easily.

"One thing I don't get, though," Mom said. "About Emilio. Yes, I can imagine him fencing paintings. He'd justify it as ensuring stewardship of the art with the chance to turn a buck. However, re-homing the odd Pissarro isn't the same as killing someone." She shook her head. "No, I don't see Emilio getting blood on his hands, and I certainly can't imagine him stooping to poison-pen letters."

"Sam agrees." After having witnessed Emilio at the guesthouse, I had to agree, too. Writing petty anonymous letters to extort twenty dollars a pop wasn't his style, and neither was anything as messy as murder. The sheriff's office would tell us for sure, but for now I couldn't help but believe the murderer was still out there.

We were back to square one. I lay awake most of the night, dipping into fitful sleep only to dream of blood-stained letters and Sam's stony expression. My parents were headed to divorce, unless I could do something. Sam presumably still pondered the knowledge that his girlfriend could talk to books and move them through the air like homing pigeons, and I had no idea if he could ever accept it.

Adding to my misery, I hadn't been able to track down the writer of the poison-pen letters—a malicious busybody who might also be a murderer. Or was I wrong about that? I'd assumed that the letters were cover for a larger crime. After all, they cited ridiculously minor misdeeds, except perhaps for whatever the situation was between Patty and Darla. Then there was my own letter. The question remained of how the writer of the letters got the information they needed.

When first light broke, I was tangled in damp sheets. I kicked them off as I heard Sam's SUV pull out of his driveway, and I leapt to the window to catch his taillights winking in the dawn. What was he thinking about? It was too early to expect a call or text, and there was no telling how busy he'd be today, especially given the enormity of Emilio Landau's arrest and the trail of art thieves it might uncover.

Rodney lay in the windowsill, catching what he could of the cooler air.

"Good morning, baby." I stroked his glossy fur and knelt to kiss him between the ears. "What am I going to do?"

From downstairs, the full-throated trill of the library's old phones sounded. Without a doubt, spam. Anyone who needed me outside work hours would call my cell phone. I envisioned the phone's hulking form and its heavy handset. A holdover from the days of party lines.

My hand froze on Rodney's back. Could it really be that simple?

A sigh from my nightstand drew my attention to a book that had appeared overnight. I clicked on my bedside lamp. *It Takes a Village: And Other Lessons Children Teach Us* was the library's choice for my attention. It takes a village. I rested a hand on the book's cover as a mental light bulb illuminated. Yes, a village.

"Thank you, books," I whispered and glanced at the clock. It was early here, but back East people would be making coffee and shaking breakfast cereal into bowls. I made a few calls. Then I set to getting dressed.

I had a poison-pen letter writer to find, and all of Wilfred was going to help.

CHAPTER THIRTY-TWO

Darla had been generous in letting me take over the café's patio. "If you don't mind the heat," she'd told me. She sniffed the air. "And a bit of smoke."

True, heat would mount during the day, but for the moment the patio was relatively cool, thanks to its roof and the breeze over the meadow. As for the air, wildfire smoke was notorious for blowing in from even hundreds of miles away, and surely a shift in the wind would bring fresh air soon. I'd spread the word about a town meeting using the two most effective methods I knew: telling Patty and buying several dozen donuts from the Do It Donut the next town over. Darla didn't mind the off-site donuts since she knew it would boost coffee sales.

My goal was simple: Flush out the poison-pen writer. Anyone nosy enough to have catalogued the town's sins was certainly going to attend. All I had to do was egg them on to reveal themselves. I had mapped what should be a foolproof strategy.

By ten in the morning, a crowd had gathered on the café's patio, and the several dozen donuts I'd brought were rapidly disappearing. I was happy to see Patty at the crowd's edge, despite her tiff with Darla. Even Adam and Lucy had come. I couldn't imagine they were on the Wilfred grapevine, but it wouldn't be unusual that they were breakfasting at the café or driving through town and caught wind of the impromptu meeting.

Lalena sat near me with Sailor on her lap and Ian next to her. Helen Garlington patted powdered sugar from her lips. She'd stopped by before her organ lesson at eleven up at the library. Ruth Littlewood was here, of course. Even Buffy and Thor lingered near their grandmother. Thor's cape must be hot in this weather, but he refused to surrender it. No Babe Hamilton, which was a relief. Until I sorted out the mystery of the interfering magic, I planned to keep her at arm's length.

Ellie Wallingford was missing. I'd grown used to her baton-twirling antics across the street as she tried to rile Darla. She must still be grounded.

I stood. "Thank you, everyone, for coming." Wilfredians watched me silently. "I have a huge lead on the poison-pen letter writer." Ruth Littlewood looked up from fidgeting with her binoculars. Lalena smiled in encouragement. "It has to do with the town's party line."

Helen Garlington harrumphed, and Mother Tohler shot her a dirty look. The notoriously prolific Tohler clan must have been big talkers.

I continued. "Until twenty years ago, loops of party lines circled through town. When the mill shut down and Wilfred shrank, the system dwindled to just two lines. After looking at the letters and talking with people who'd received them, I determined a couple of things. First, the secrets in the letters date to when the party lines were in existence." This drew nods and murmurs from the crowd. "Second, most stemmed from one loop of a dozen homes."

Duke, apparently here between jobs, stood and adjusted his tool belt. "But some of the so-called crimes involved people on different lines. Me, for example. I was busted for fishing without a license, but Darla, on the other line, got called out for something else." He glanced at Patty, who dipped her head. Whatever it was between the sisters really needed to be resolved.

"Did you happen to talk about your catch with someone on the other party line?" I asked. Duke nodded slowly and sat down again. "That's all it would take. Anyone listening in would know." I opened my notebook to show the list of anonymous letters and the columns of people on each party line with a web of lines connecting them. I'd spent the first few hours of the day with graph paper and an old telephone directory. "My mother is going to take this to each of you who received a letter. Could you confirm which party line you were on and who you might have talked to, if anyone, about the crime you were accused of?"

Nods and shrugs settled over the patio. Patty edged away. Not to worry—I'd get to her later.

"One more thing," I said. This was the big one. "I've made another deduction. The poison-pen letters and Benjamin Duffy's murder are linked."

Murmurs floated through the crowd. Several Wilfredians stood, jaws agape, donuts in hand.

"Oh, come on," Ruth Littlewood said. "The letters were spiteful and got us riled up, but they're small potatoes compared to the murder."

I gestured toward the table with Lucy and Adam Duffy. "Lucy brought Sam a letter her husband had received. It's obvious the letter writer wanted people to believe the letter drove Benjamin Duffy to relapse and fall to his death." I lowered my voice. "I'm sorry, Lucy, to bring this up." I'd warned her before our meeting, but this still couldn't be easy.

She looked at her lap, one hand resting on her belly. "It's okay. Whatever helps to find who killed Benjamin."

"I believe the other letters were cover. The poison-pen letter writer and the murderer are one and the same." This was sheer bravado, but from the looks on people's faces, intriguing if not convincing.

At first, the patio was silent. The chop-chop-chop of a helicopter sounded in the distance, probably on the alert for fire. Then discussion began, quietly at first, then more loudly.

"Ridiculous," Duke said. "Writing letters is one thing and pushing a fellow to his death is another."

Mrs. Garlington shook her head. "I simply can't believe it."

"Where did this idea come from?" Lalena asked.

Now to drop the big one. "Unless the anonymous letter writer can prove otherwise, that's the theory I'm presenting to the sheriff."

Mrs. Tohler stood and crossed her meaty arms over

her chest. She narrowed her eyes in a gesture that let us know no one would accuse her offspring of being murderers.

Meanwhile, Mom circled the tables, double-checking my work with the party line chart.

I had successfully stirred the pot, and now it was time to open the library. I would park myself at Circulation and wait. If the poison-pen letter writer was not the murderer, they surely couldn't let this stand. Before the day was out, I was certain I'd know who that person was. Either that, or my worst imaginings were true, and the letter writer and murderer truly were one and the same.

Hours later, I threw down my pen in frustration. Nothing. It hadn't worked. I was so sure I could incite the anonymous letter writer to reveal themself by calling them a murderer, but my attempts to shake them from the bushes had failed. The bright side of this morning's exercise was that the letters did appear to be connected to the party lines. Each of the incidents in the letters could be linked to a call to or from someone on party line A.

But no confession. Now what?

Compounding matters, Sam hadn't called. A glance at his driveway showed he wasn't home, either. How long would it take until I'd discover that he'd never call? That he couldn't accept my magic or having a witch in his life? I hoped he was merely occupied with the Emilio Landau case, if not Benjamin Duffy's murder.

"Cupcakes," Ruth Littlewood said, snapping me to attention.

"I'm sorry. You're hungry?" I replied.

"No. This isn't a bakery. I need a cupcake to read. Something with little nutritional value."

This earned a Bronx cheer from Popular Fiction. From day one of being a librarian I'd learned that reading carried a lot of baggage, especially among people who didn't read a lot. The same folks who happily devoured television sitcoms and ate frozen pizzas might stick their noses in the air about their reading material, stating that they read only nonfiction or literary works. To me, this was not discernment. This was snobbery. A good story was a good story. Period.

I posed my hands on my hips. "We have gripping novels, if that's what you mean. Books sure to engross you and have you turning pages."

"Exactly what I need. There's a wildfire watch, and I'll be next to my radio waiting for a call for the volunteer fire department. I need something distracting."

Ruth Littlewood didn't actually fight fires anymore, but she was one of our local dispatchers. Duke kept Wilfred's vintage fire truck in such fine condition that it was regularly requested for local parades.

I gathered an Ann Cleeves mystery featuring birdwatchers George and Molly Palmer-Jones and a few Donna Andrews bird-themed cozies for her. As Ruth left, Buffy and Thor scampered in from the atrium and made their way straight to me.

"Nice try to find the person writing those letters," Buffy said. Today she wore a pale pink T-shirt featuring a unicorn with a flowing mane and the words *Dreams Come True* in script.

Thor, in his usual cape, added, "Perhaps you need assistance."

"For a low, low price," Buffy said.

"Kids can go anywhere, do just about anything." Thor spread his hands wide in full sales mode.

Buffy stooped to pet Rodney. "As long as Grandma doesn't find out."

"Your current methods have failed. You need us," Thor said.

Both children faced me, dollar signs in their eyes. Sadly, they weren't wrong. "What can you do for me?"

"Spy," Buffy said promptly.

"Spy on whom?" I asked.

"Your prime suspects." Buffy spoke patiently, as if to someone a little slow to understand.

Behind her, Adam Duffy had entered and smiled. This was official library work. I signaled that I'd be with him in a moment. "I admire your entrepreneurial spirit, but what is it you think you'll find? You're not going to peek in a window and see someone cutting letters from a magazine."

Buffy's eyes widened. Thor nudged her and shook his head. "Don't tell."

"Don't tell what?" I asked.

"I told you she was too cheap to help out a couple of poor little children," Thor said and shot me a dirty look. "Let's see if Duke and Desmond need something."

"No," Buffy said. "They always give us messy things to do. I don't want to get my shirt greasy."

"Maybe Ellie has another idea," Thor said. He glanced at the mantel clock. "She should be done being grounded by now."

He and Buffy hurried out the door, leaving me with Adam, who'd turned his head to watch their exit. "Thank you for waiting," I said. "I adore those two and their hustles, but they're an acquired taste. How can I help you?"

"They're looking for Ellie Wallingford?"

I nodded. "Apparently she's their ringleader for money-making ideas."

"They won't find her at home. I just saw her with some friends headed for Forest Grove."

"They'll survive," I said. "They'll find someone's dog to wash or lawn to mow. Poorly. Can I help you?"

"Yes," Adam said. "That is, I don't know what resource will be best, but, as I told you, Lucy and I want to sell the Aerie. Now that Emilio Landau's out of the picture, we'll have to put it on the market." Although his words said "sell," his expression showed regret.

"You love the Aerie," I said.

He took a deep breath, the kind of inhale that expresses more than words might. "It's time to move on. Lucy doesn't want to live there, and I need to get away, too. The Aerie holds too many bad memories."

"I have an idea." An idea that would serve Adam as well as keep Mom occupied. "My mother's a real estate agent. She's upstairs reading. How about if I ask her to give you an overview of the process of buying and selling? She might have tactics to suggest."

"You don't think she'd mind?"

"I know she wouldn't. She likes to keep busy." I

picked up the heavy desk phone to buzz upstairs, then rested it again in its cradle without calling. "The Aerie was on one of the party lines."

"True," he said. "I learned a lot more about the Tohlers than I ever wanted, all in two-second snippets." He laughed. Instead of lighting up his expression, his smile only deepened his face's tired lines.

I had a hard time imagining Adam listening in and jotting down the salacious details of conversations, then saving them to shake twenty dollar bills out of Wilfredians two decades later. He'd inherited enough money to live comfortably, so greed couldn't be a motivator. I could safely cross him off the list of poison-pen letter writers.

I picked up the phone again. "I'll get Mom for you."

Once my mother had led Adam into the kitchen to talk real estate, I turned over our conversation in my mind. Who did need money in Wilfred? Could that be a clue to the anonymous letter writer's identity? Everyone needed cash, I supposed, to some extent. I grabbed my notebook and examined the entries. A couple of dozen letters at twenty dollars each came to a bit more than four hundred dollars.

Four hundred dollars wasn't anything to sneeze at— Buffy and Thor would sell their grandmother for that kind of cash—but it wouldn't be enough to cover a car's brake job or a root canal. Then the answer came to me. It was so obvious that I was ashamed I hadn't thought of it earlier. Ellie Wallingford. Four hundred dollars would go a long way toward covering majorette camp. However, she wasn't even born when some of the deeds in the letters took place, and she certainly didn't live here when Wilfred was on party lines. How could she have known what to put into poison-pen letters?

The books from Reverend Duffy's house. I remembered the phone on the Reverend's desk at the church and the hissing of his crated books at the Aerie. I closed my eyes and could easily imagine him seated in his black leather chair, a tumbler of whiskey at his elbow, carefully lifting the phone's receiver and jotting what he'd heard into a ledger. He needed some measure of the town's wickedness—why, I had no idea. It would have been after his last entry, the entry where he'd promised his dead wife he "wouldn't let it happen again." Whatever "it" was.

Who's to say Ellie didn't find those records among the books her parents had bought for the guesthouse? Coached by her conversations on entrepreneurship with Emilio, she might have seen the possibilities to raise camp expenses. There was certainly no love lost between her and the rest of town.

Buffy and Thor had told me they'd done work for Ellie. Secret work. Could it have been gluing letters onto paper?

I stood. There was one way to find out. I picked up my desk phone and punched the button for the book binding room. "Roz? Could you cover the front desk?"

CHAPTER THIRTY-THREE

I found Buffy and Thor at the Magnolia Rolling Estates tucking flyers behind screen doors. A flyer slipped from Buffy's stash, and I picked it up. The top featured a crayon drawing of two stick figures, one with billowing yellow hair and the other with a cape. The flyer read, *Odd jobs for a reesonable fee*. I hoped copy editing wasn't one of those odd jobs. *Car wash, dog walk, entertaynment* were listed as options.

It was just after midday, but already the heat was clearly getting to them. Thor dragged his heels and kicked up gravel, raising dust.

"Buffy, Thor," I called after them.

Buffy turned first. Her expression perked up. "You have a job for us?"

I handed her the dropped flyer. "Not exactly. I have questions."

Thor sat on the shady ground under the trellis of roses surrounding Lalena's PALM READINGS sign. "What?"

"One dollar per question," Buffy quickly added.

"Only if you guarantee an answer." I, too, moved to the shade. Today would be a scorcher.

A wily look crossed Buffy's face. "We can give answers, all right."

"The truth," I amended. "Or no cash."

Buffy and Thor exchanged glances. The heat must have gotten to them, because Thor reluctantly nodded. "The truth or no money," he agreed.

"What did you do for Ellie?" I asked.

"Try another question," Buffy said.

"That's my question," I said. "That's what I need to know. It's important. Really important."

"She made us promise not to tell," Thor said. "Can't you ask us something else?"

I dug in my purse and produced my wallet. No cash there. Back I went into my purse, this time for the emergency twenty-dollar bill I kept in a side pocket. I unfolded the bill, letting the "20" reveal itself slowly to Buffy and Thor's eager gazes.

"Now can you tell me?" I'd make it even easier. "I bet you were cutting words from a magazine and pasting them into letters."

Buffy swallowed, and Thor said, "Yes."

"You were helping Ellie make anonymous letters."

"I don't know anything about that," Buffy said, her eyes still on the twenty-dollar bill. "Thor only said yes. He could have meant anything."

I pulled the bill to my chest. "I need the answer to my question."

Thor cracked first. "That's the answer." He snatched at the bill and I released it. "Yes, we were gluing stuff for her."

"Thor, we promised not to tell!" Buffy stamped her foot.

"What? She only gave us ten dollars. Besides, Josie guessed."

Twenty dollars well spent. It was true: Ellie Wallingford had written the poison-pen letters. She hadn't been at the café this morning to defend herself, because she had been grounded. By now she likely knew the anonymous letter writer—her—was also suspected of being a murderer.

The warmth of satisfaction settled over me, and it wasn't the summer heat, either. Now all I had to do was to find Ellie and extract a confession, and the poison-pen mystery would be solved.

Adam Duffy had told me he'd seen Ellie bound for Forest Grove. Wilfred was so small that it wasn't unusual for people to travel the ten minutes to Gaston or twenty to Forest Grove for dentist appointments or even to do their weekly shopping. The P.O., while convenient, carried an idiosyncratic selection of groceries. For instance, the owner refused to stock mayonnaise. He didn't like it, and he told shoppers he didn't want it in his store.

Ellie's parents would know when she'd be home. Surely her mother or father would be working at the guesthouse, even if the other parent had chauffeured Ellie to her errand.

The guesthouse's foyer was refreshing after the hot afternoon. Over the summer, I'd quickly considered the cost and disruption of having air conditioning installed in the library, then dismissed it as quickly. The library's trustees would pooh-pooh the idea, saying the old mansion hadn't needed it so far, and the trees kept it cool enough. Not to mention what it would cost. Here, though, the roses in the vase on the entry hall table were crisp, and the cool air held no hint of smoke.

Ellie's mother emerged from the drawing room. "Josie. It's nice to see you under better circumstances. Can you believe we were harboring an international art fence?"

"It was a shock," I said. "Did the investigators cause a lot of hassle?" We'd seen them lunching at the café in their suits. Buffy and Thor had tried to hire themselves out for guided tours of Wilfred.

"They took over the entire upstairs. Still haven't left. The upside is that we've rented them rooms at the government per diem." She straightened the vase. "How can I help you?"

"I wondered if you could tell me when Ellie is expected home?"

Janet Wallingford's eyes narrowed. "Why? What has she been up to now?"

Ellie's mother should know if her daughter had masterminded a town-wide extortion scheme, but I didn't feel comfortable sharing my suspicions until I'd confirmed them. "It has to do with a project she and Buffy and Thor did."

Janet Wallingford nodded but raised an eyebrow in suspicion. "Nothing at the library?"

"No." Why had she asked that?

She smiled, seemingly in relief. "I remember the

project with the kids. Last week. They were upstairs in Ellie's room for a full afternoon. As for when she'll be home, I'm not sure. I'll give you her phone number, and you can text her if you don't run into her first."

I tapped Ellie's digits into my phone as her mother recited them. "Will she be gone all day, do you think? The traffic from Forest Grove can get busy in the afternoon."

Ellie's mother cocked her head. "Forest Grove? She didn't say anything about that, and she wouldn't leave town without telling me. No, she planned to ride her bicycle to the library. That's why I mentioned it. Should I tell her you're looking for her?"

Adam Duffy had told me he'd seen Ellie and had specifically noted Forest Grove. Why would he say that? She certainly hadn't been at the library. "Yes, thank you," I said, distracted by the thoughts now tangling in my mind. "When did she leave?"

Her mother shrugged. "Just after lunch. Say, an hour ago."

In the guesthouse's front yard, I texted Ellie. I waited a minute, but the screen of my phone was still, except for its cover photo of Rodney lying on his back, giving me the stink eye.

I slipped my phone into my pocket to better hear a reply text should it come. Either Ellie had hidden her destination from her mother, or she'd changed plans. That, or Adam Duffy had lied to me. I started my walk up the hill to the library.

Yesterday Ellie had thrown a fit when I'd mentioned Benjamin Duffy's letter and the possible link to his murder. If, as I suspected, Ellie had written the letters herself—or, rather, art-directed Buffy and Thor to do it—she'd know if Benjamin had truly received a letter.

I halted. *Oh no.*

If, say, the letter had gone to Adam, and Adam had seen the opportunity to shift suspicion of Benjamin's death toward the anonymous letter writer by claiming Benjamin had received the letter instead of him, then had Lucy deliver it to Sam . . .

Surely Ellie wouldn't be foolish enough to confront Adam. Or would she?

I had to get to the Aerie, and right away.

CHAPTER THIRTY-FOUR

I hurried up the hill, over the river to the library, moisture gathering on my brow and smoke-tinged air burning in my lungs. Adam was still inside the library—I recognized his Subaru. I could confront him.

But what good would that do me? All I had in the way of evidence was that he'd lied to me about where Ellie was. That Ellie had figured out he'd also lied about Benjamin receiving a poison-pen letter was conjecture on my part. However, I had no proof. It wasn't enough to get the sheriff's office's attention.

Furthermore, Ellie's life was more important than apprehending Adam.

I started up the Corolla and rolled down its windows, cursing the car's lack of air conditioning. It was a three-mile drive to the Aerie. A long way on a bicycle, especially in this heat, but if her yelling last night was any indicator, Ellie had been determined. Farmhouses and meadows sloping to the river passed by my windows with basalt foothills in the distance. Today the landscape, normally so seductive, barely registered to me.

A story began to come together in my mind. Adam may have been resentful of the years he spent taking care of his cantankerous father while Benjamin lived in New York, making music and free to do as he wished. I could see that. Years of living under the reverend's silent judgment, years of bending to his not-so-silent commands. Now the Reverend Duffy was dead. All Adam wanted was to sell the Aerie and to begin a real life. Emilio Landau had appeared, cash in hand. It must have felt like a miracle.

Then Benjamin showed up. To Benjamin, the Aerie was a home far from the city's temptations and full of happy memories. He could raise his children there and show them a different life than the one he'd lived. Lucy wasn't a fan, but Benjamin had probably figured she'd come around. Eventually she'd love Marlin Hill's wild beauty and strange, alluring ghost-town vibe as much as he did.

Adam couldn't stand for that. Who was Benjamin, the prodigal son, to appear after more than a decade away and thwart his plans? Where had Benjamin been when their father was shouting for his coffee or had shut himself into the church office? Benjamin was incommunicado, partying in New York, that's where. Adam must have figured a quick push off the deck would solve his problems for good.

However, Adam was supposed to be at a doctor's appointment in Forest Grove. Lucy had confirmed it. Yet she'd also said she'd waited for the doctor, and she didn't mention Adam waiting with her. It would only take an hour for him to rush to Marlin Hill, kill his brother, and be back in Forest Grove in time to pick up Lucy with a story about window shopping or having to stop by the high school.

The smoke in the air was thickening. I rolled up my windows.

Driving into Marlin Hill was like climbing into a cave of fir trees. I shifted down. The air cooled, and the broad view of countryside narrowed to a rutted, tree-lined road with long-abandoned lanes leading to similarly abandoned homes. I was literally at the end of the line. Before me, Marlin Hill was a circle of road with a boarded-up general store and the pristine white shape of the church.

I took a hard left and climbed the drive to the Aerie. Dust covered the brush bordering the lane. I cheered at the sight of pink metal jutting from a clump of Oregon grape. Ellie's bicycle. She was here.

I had barely yanked the Corolla into park when I was out the door and pounding on the Aerie's front door. "Ellie?" I tried the knob. Locked.

I shielded my eyes against the sun and looked up at the house's sheer walls. In the distance sounded the buzz of plane engines. Firefighters, hopefully far down the valley.

"Ellie!"

No response. Adam had killed once. Had he killed again? If I was careful, I could peer over the cliff's drop.

I edged down the slope, grabbing at brush to slow my descent. My foot hit a slick of gravel, and I slid, flailing, until I caught one of the Aerie's stout supports.

I closed my eyes and fought to regain my breath. Below me, the crevasse gaped with the dry riverbed below. *Please let Ellie be alive*, I prayed silently.

A glint of metal in the gravel caught my eye. A baton. Ellie must have lost it. From a window above me came the sound of fists pounding. She must be locked upstairs.

Relief and frustration flowed over me simultaneously. Ellie was here, but she was shut into the house more than three stories above me, and I was stuck grasping a wooden post on a gravel-blanketed slope. What could I do?

If I leaned back—still holding the support column—I could just about make out Ellie's pale skin pressed against the window of what must have been Adam's and Benjamin's mother's room.

"Josie!" Ellie yelled from another window closer to me, likely a bathroom window. This one opened, but it was too small to climb through, even for a lithe teenager. Not that squeezing through the window would have done her any good. A drop that far could be fatal. "I'm locked up here."

Then I had an idea. I closed my eyes and focused my energy. Yes. It just might work. "Go to the other room and break the window."

"How?"

"Find something. Anything. Use it to smash out the window."

"No," she whined. "Can't you get me out instead?"

She was stubborn. And infuriating. But maybe . . . "I'm going to throw you the baton."

The baton was a man's length from me, up the slope.

I gingerly lowered myself to all fours and crawled to it, keeping clumps of brush and jutting rock in my peripheral vision to grasp if needed. At last, I had the baton in hand.

"Stick your arms out the window. I'm tossing it to you." I coughed against the smoke, thicker now. I rose carefully to standing, and holding the baton from its end as I'd seen Ellie do so many times, I hurled it toward the bathroom window.

Ellie grasped at it, but the baton was a good six inches from her hands. It fell to the ground and bounced once. I barely caught it before it bounded down the hill.

"Haven't you ever thrown a baton before?" Ellie said.

"I'm trying to save your life here. Hold on."

I centered myself, planted my feet as firmly as I could manage, and tossed the baton. Once again I missed my mark. This time I wasn't so lucky, and the baton hit the ground, flopped to its side and rolled. I flailed for it, but couldn't lose my footing. It wouldn't serve either Ellie or me if I fell to the same fate as Benjamin.

I held my breath as the baton came to rest against the house's support pillar. Again I lowered myself to all fours and backed down the hill to pick up the baton. Gravel raked at my knees.

"Hurry," Ellie said from above. "I can see smoke. Lots of it."

I followed her gaze. From down here, I didn't make out billows, but the afternoon darkened to gray. *Please*, I willed the baton. *Please find your way to Ellie. She needs you.* If only it had been a book. Tears of frustration gathered in my eyes.

I hurled the baton upward, and Ellie—stretching her arm as far as it could reach, face pressed sideways against the glass—grasped it and pulled it into the house.

I let out a long breath. "Now use your baton to smash out the bigger window. The picture window in the next room."

"Then what?"

Relief. As I'd hoped, her baton had given her courage. "Never mind that right now. Just smash out the window." I crawled backward, out of the range of falling glass.

Never had the sound of a shattering window been so welcome. As Ellie thrust her baton with clean, strong motions, I centered my energy to flow up the house, into the window. I felt the books in the room—mostly paperback romances, not the solid hardbacks I'd have preferred for my task—and let their energy bond with mine. The romances fed me stories of strength, of slapped dukes and midnight elopements, of escapes from arranged marriages.

"Okay!" Ellie shouted. "Hurry!"

"Do you see the books in the room with you? Throw them out the window." For once, I was grateful for Ellie's penchant for fibbing. What I was about to do wouldn't be believed by anyone.

"What? Who cares about saving some stupid books. What about me?"

"We don't have much time." I coughed again against the smoke. "Do as I say and throw the books."

Ellie froze and looked at me. Then she disappeared into the room. Seconds later, an armload of flimsy paperbacks sailed from the window with shouts of *whee!* only I could hear.

I steeled down on my energy. "Books! Make a staircase."

The books froze from their free fall and hovered midair. One by one, they fell into steps two feet apart. There weren't enough books yet to reach the window. Ellie stared, her mouth open.

"That's not all the books." I sensed more inside, thrilling to join the others. "Throw out the rest."

Again Ellie disappeared, and again she tossed the books out the window to complete the stairs. The final novel, a Barbara Cartland romance, crowned the staircase's top. It ended three feet below the window, but it would have to do.

"Now put a blanket over the window frame and lower yourself out," I commanded.

Ellie stood, staring.

"Do it! We don't have much time."

The helicopters were louder now. If we didn't hurry, I wasn't sure we could make it out of the Aerie, let alone Marlin Hill. Thankfully, Ellie obeyed. She draped a quilt over the windowsill jagged with broken glass and slid out feet first on her belly, one hand grasping the baton, the other holding the window frame. Her toes felt for the top step of books.

"Hurry!" I yelled. There hadn't been enough books to make a handrail. I counted on her agility and strength to get her down.

As she descended, the books forming the top steps

dropped to lower stairs to firm and widen them. It worked. At last Ellie reached the ground.

"What just happened?" she said.

"Never mind that. Come on. Careful—we'll have to crawl."

Ellie refused to relinquish her baton. I understood. It was her security blanket, just as the books were mine. We made it up the slope and jumped into the car. I popped the trunk and started the engine.

"What are you waiting for?" Ellie said. "I saw the fire. Go!"

She burst into tears. As she sobbed—relief? Fear? A little of both?—flying books stacked themselves into my trunk. It was the least I owed them.

We set down the road, driving to beat the fire.

CHAPTER THIRTY-FIVE

Ellie was safe, but our trial was not yet over. To exit the Aerie's side road, I had no choice but to drive toward the fire. Even with windows rolled up tight, my lungs choked and eyes burned. And now the flames were visible as raging orange patches crowned with black.

Beside me, Ellie cried in long, hiccupping sobs. For all her bluster, she was still a kid, I reminded myself. She'd gotten herself—and by extension, me—into a situation far more perilous than she could have ever imagined.

I realized Ellie was trying to tell me something. I kept my hands tight on the steering wheel. "What?"

"My . . . my bike," she said between sobs.

I didn't reply. I couldn't. The smoke wove an opaque curtain, and it took everything I had to see even a few feet in front of the car. A wrong turn and we could career right off the same cliff I'd worked so hard to avoid just a quarter hour earlier.

"My bicycle is gone forever!" she wailed.

"We'll be gone forever if I can't get us out of here. I can barely see."

Panic overtook Ellie's grief at losing her bicycle. Her tears ceased. "Can't you go any faster?"

"Not safely." Although it wasn't safe to drive so slowly, either. Flames leapfrogged the road, making a curious patchwork of fire and green. We both screamed. The fire briefly illuminated the church. It caught like a scrap of newspaper.

I felt something from the trunk. In my mind, a map unfolded. "Ellie, was there a map among the books?"

"I don't know," she wailed.

In two seconds, veer left, came a voice. A book's voice, authoritative and matter-of-fact. My heart leapt. I couldn't second-guess the map's instructions. If we were to survive, I would have to trust its directions, and I would have to accelerate.

"Where are you going?" Ellie asked. "You can't see! Slow down!"

Stay straight for the count of five, then a sharp right. Four, three, two, one, turn.

I turned. The car was hot enough to roast us alive.

What next? I asked silently.

Three seconds, turn left.

I turned again.

Not so sharply. Now drive straight for two-point-two miles.

I stepped on the gas. We were leaving the fire behind, and the gray around us thinned. I could see to drive, but it was still too smoky to open the windows. Only now that it was draining away could I feel the adrenaline that had suffused me. I nearly cried with relief. For a moment, I simply enjoyed the silence.

Ellie broke the quiet. "What happened back there?"

"What do you mean?" I knew exactly what she meant.

"The books. You told me to throw them out the window, and they made a staircase."

"That's crazy talk," I said. "It's natural you'd imagine things, given the situation. Let's talk about something real, like those letters you wrote."

"The books were totally real. They hung in the air. I could put my whole weight on them."

"The letters, Ellie." I was confident no one would believe her tale of flying books.

Two state-run fire vehicles raced past us, followed by Wilfred's vintage fire truck, Desmond and Duke in the front seat. Marlin Hill would be in ashes by now, including the Aerie.

"I never sent the dead guy a letter. Adam Duffy said I had. He lied so people would think I was a murderer. I was not. I just wanted to get some money for majorette camp."

"Did it ever occur to you that Adam Duffy might be the murderer, and that's why he wanted to shift the blame to the person who wrote the letters?" Had he known that person was an impulsive teenager, he might have acted differently. "What did he say to you when you confronted him?"

I didn't need to look over to know Ellie had stuck out her lower lip in a pout. "Nothing. He grabbed my arm and twisted it behind my back and shoved me up those steps and locked the door. It hurt."

"Nothing at all?"

"Just that he'd be back. I yelled, but he drove away. That jerk. He was so mean to me."

I shivered to think of what he might have done had he returned. As it was, he was likely thanking fate for the wildfire at Marlin Hill, figuring his dirty work had been taken care of for him. He was surely long gone by now. I'd made the choice to save Ellie rather than go after Adam. It had been the right choice. I glanced at Ellie, still clearly more upset with Adam than with the havoc she'd wreaked in town, not to mention the hell she'd put me through.

"Now I don't even have enough money for camp," she moaned.

"Ellie, do you have any idea what you've done? You've made dozens of people miserable, not to mention endangering both of our lives." I hoped her parents would give her a fitting punishment. Grounding her until she reached the age of majority would be a start.

We were coming into Wilfred. I slowed to make the turn into the library's driveway. Sam's SUV wasn't at Big House, and a quick glance at my phone showed he hadn't called or texted, either. I'd need to call him right away to tell him about Adam Duffy. He'd want to send out an APB. Adam could be on a plane to Costa Rica at this very moment.

As I pulled in, Mom emerged from the library's side

door and hurried to the car. She glanced at Ellie, then to me. "Honey, are you okay?"

I gulped fresh air and nodded.

"I need to talk to you," Mom said.

"Can it wait a bit? I have to—"

"No. Right now."

From the set of her lips, Mom was serious. I turned to Ellie. "Could you wait here for a second?"

"I want to go home," she said.

I understood. She'd been through a lot in the past few hours: confronting a murderer, getting kidnapped, being rescued by magic, and outrunning a wildfire. "I promise to take you home as soon as I've talked to my mother. Why don't you stretch your legs for a minute?"

Ellie looked at me with suspicion and opened the passenger door. She tossed her baton in the air, where it twirled and landed in her hand, light as a tossed rose stem.

Mom gestured to me to follow her out of Ellie's range of hearing. "It's about Adam Duffy."

I drew back. "What about him?"

"He's upstairs."

I let this sink in a moment. Upstairs? A murderer? "I thought for sure he'd be out of town by now. I, he . . ." I nodded toward Ellie, who tossed her baton and danced on the lawn with violence and grace. Poor kid.

"I know," Mom said. "We were talking real estate, and I got the feeling something was off about him. While I was explaining to Adam how he could negotiate a bridge sale to buy something new while the Aerie was on the market, I couldn't shake visions of him in strange situations. They passed like photographs in a slide show, like they did the other night when we cast the spell. I saw him looking over the broken railing on the deck. I saw him pulling an envelope—clearly another poison-pen letter—from the table next to his bed and hiding it in the back pocket of a pair of jeans." Her breath quickened. "The worst—the worst was seeing him push Ellie up the stairs and bolt the door. That's when I knew."

"Knew what?" I whispered.

"Knew he'd pushed his brother off the railing. I heard music, Josie. They were playing music, and Adam pushed him. He must have taken the instruments away and doctored the scene with whiskey."

Mom had been using her magic. Something did seem different about her—despite her worry, she glowed. She'd cut the self-imposed bonds on her magic.

"You say Adam is here?" As I spoke, I reached for my phone to call the sheriff's office.

"Upstairs. He'd seemed eager to leave, but someone stopped by saying Marlin Hill was on fire. He said he'd stay until he found out if the Aerie survived."

He probably thought the stars were aligned to take care of Ellie for him. As for the Aerie, at least he'd have insurance money. Or so he'd thought.

"I'm calling 9-1-1." I spoke to the dispatcher and urged haste. Who knew how long Adam would be satisfied lounging in the library? The steady beat of the baton in Ellie's palms as she twirled it and caught it reminded me she was still here. I had to get her out of Adam's sight. One glance, and he'd run. Or worse.

"Ellie," I said, "I'm taking you home. Right now."

Smack. The baton found its home in her palm. "Okay." She slid into the passenger seat.

I glanced up at the library's second floor, home to Local History, and saw a face near the window. Adam Duffy. I was too late.

CHAPTER THIRTY-SIX

I froze. Should I rush Ellie out of the way and risk Adam escaping? Or should I hold on, knowing sheriff's deputies were on their way to apprehend him?

"I want to go home, Ellie said. Tears streaked the soot on her face, and she clutched her baton to her chest.

Once again, I was reminded she was still a kid. "I'm so sorry, but we can't leave now. I'll call your mom to come hang out with you." The sheriff's office would probably require it, anyway. "But you'll need to tell the deputy what Adam Duffy did to you."

"Then I'm getting out of the car."

"No, Ellie, stay inside. With the doors locked." I had a clear view of the library's front, side, and kitchen doors. Once the deputies arrived, Adam might make a run for it, and I didn't want Ellie dangled as a hostage. He showed no sign of leaving—at least, not yet. I didn't want to freak out Ellie further by telling her Adam was nearby.

Her lower lip edged forward. "Everything? Do I have to tell about the letters?"

"There's no way around it," I said as I shot off a text to her mother.

Ellie stared at me a moment, then defiantly opened the door and returned to the lawn. "I'm not waiting in that hot car."

She hurled her baton in the air. Her face impassive, she turned 180 degrees and caught the baton on its descent, whirled it around her waist, and thrust it again into the air, among the branches of the oak trees. It was strangely beautiful, her grace in the face of her pain.

"Ellie, you need to wait in the car. It's not safe out here."

"Why not?" Her lower lip protruded once again.

"Because—"

Before I could warn her, I was interrupted by the kitchen door bursting open. Pushing Mom out of the way, Adam Duffy emerged. With a knife in his fist.

Ellie halted, her eyes widening.

Adam approached, and I backed against the Corolla. Sun glinted from the knife's blade. "Hand me the keys," he said in a low voice.

I fumbled in my pocket to do as he commanded. *Come on, sheriff deputies*, I silently urged.

"You locked me up!" Ellie yelled at Adam. "You'll pay for it, you liar. You left me to die."

At last I had the keys. I offered them to Adam, but he'd turned to Ellie and raised his knife to chest height, tip thrust out. He moved forward. I lunged toward him, but he was just beyond my grasp.

Without a change in expression, Ellie lowered her

baton. And tripped Adam Duffy. He fell flat, the knife a foot from his hand. I pounced on it.

At the same time, a sheriff's SUV pulled into the library's drive. Two deputies, strangers to me, alit from the vehicle. Ellie's mother was right behind them. She'd wasted no time jumping into the family car and driving the short distance up the hill.

Mom had taken the seconds between Adam's exit from the library and his attempt on Ellie to grab a cast-iron skillet from the kitchen. She now held it over Adam's head.

"Honey!" Janet Wallingford clasped Ellie tightly. Ellie burst into tears once again.

The deputies watched, hands on their weapons, unsure what to do next.

"Ellie has something to tell you about Adam Duffy and his brother's murder. This is Ellie's mother. If you'd like, you can talk in the library." One of the deputies turned to Ellie.

"And this," I said, pointing to Adam, flat on the lawn, my mother still wielding the skillet over his head, "is Benjamin Duffy's murderer. He kidnapped Ellie Wallingford and left her to die."

Mom dropped the frying pan. The deputy read Adam Duffy his rights. I took a page from Ellie's book and burst into tears.

Sometime later, the deputies emerged from the library kitchen's door with Adam handcuffed between them. Ellie and her mother followed. Ellie stared at the ground, but her mother was holding the hand not clutching the baton. Ellie must have confessed about the poison-pen letters, and right now her mother cared more about getting her daughter home safely than determining what punishment she merited. I understood.

I caught one of the deputies before he ducked into the SUV. "Have you seen Sam Wilfred?"

The deputy clearly had more important things on his mind. "Wilfred's on the Landau art fencing case. In D.C. by now, I expect." He pulled the door shut between us, signaling that our conversation was over.

I backed away. Washington, D.C. That would explain why I hadn't seen him and why the house was dark. Nicky would be at the babysitter's. Why hadn't he called?

I should be calm. I should be happy. The poison-pen letter writer had been unmasked and a murderer apprehended.

I was not happy.

Rodney twisted around my ankles, and I knelt to run fingers down his back. "Come on, baby. I need a bath."

CHAPTER THIRTY-SEVEN

On the patio at Darla's Café, the flames leapt higher. We all cheered.

"Careful now," Montgomery said. "The forecast promises rain, but there's no guarantee."

Duke, a fire extinguisher at the ready, stood near the barrel while Desmond dug at the fire with a poker. One by one, people dropped their anonymous letters into the barrel on top of the burning ledger.

Wilfredians were gathered tonight to put the episode of the poison-pen letters permanently to rest. Ellie had had confessed to cribbing the letters from a ledger kept by Reverend Duffy, which she'd taken from the crate of books Ian Penclosa had sold her family. However, Wilfredians were sure she was telling tales when she explained how she'd escaped the Aerie by climbing down a staircase of books suspended midair.

"They did, didn't they, Josie?" she'd pleaded with me.

"I wish I could tell you they did," I'd truthfully

replied. "You were pretty strung out. You might have imagined anything."

Dad squeezed Mom's shoulders. Yes, my father was here. After deputies had hauled Adam away, a taxi had trundled up the gravel drive with Dad inside. My mother grabbed him by the arm and tugged him inside, giving him only a moment to wave and smile at me. She later explained she'd called the night before and asked him to come to Wilfred. He'd dropped everything, including the paper he'd planned to present, to see her. It was that easy. He'd been simply waiting for her call.

He kissed my mother's cheek. I wasn't used to seeing him so openly affectionate, and I liked it. "Nora's a genuine Jehenne de Brigue," he said.

"Who?"

"Jehenne de Brigue," Mom repeated. "A fourteenth-century French witch. I read all about her upstairs—somehow a book about medieval witches showed up on my pillow. Once I explained to Gerard how the women in our family were witches just like Jehenne de Brigue was—well, maybe not exactly, but the idea is the same—he understood. It was, it was—"

"—magic." Dad smiled at his awful joke. "I only wish I could have known sooner. My three girls, too, all witches."

My heart melted. Could Sam understand me as Dad understood Mom? They'd had decades together, while our relationship was still in its early days. "Once you'd admitted it to yourself, your own magic settled in, didn't it, Mom?"

"You helped me see it, Josie. You were willing to tell Sam about your magic while I couldn't even admit my own power to myself. Our spell opened me. All I had to do was to keep my magic open—and tell your father."

Dad smiled with proprietary love. "Can you find lost objects like Jehenne de Brigue did?"

"Darling, we'll talk about that later. Maybe you can tell me more about witchcraft in medieval France?"

He beamed. Everything between them would turn out all right.

We watched the fire with satisfaction—all of us except Patty and Darla, who chatted with animation at a nearby table. One of the best parts of getting hold of the ledger was discovering that the poison-pen letter to Darla was pure fabrication. Ellie had been angry at Darla for barring her from giving baton shows at the café, so she'd invented a story about Patty making moves on Montgomery. It also explained why she'd demanded fifty rather than twenty dollars from Darla. Patty and Darla had already been edging toward a reconciliation, and Ellie's confession had sealed it.

Since Adam's arrest, I'd pondered the reverend's change in attitude after his wife's death as well as the list of transgressions he'd felt compelled to record as he listened on the party line in the church's office. A theory had formed in my mind. Emilio Landau's confession supported it.

Emilio told investigators that when he'd helped his father design the Aerie, he'd seen a young Adam Duffy push his mother from the house's unfinished deck. Emilio used this information as leverage to coerce Adam to sell. Why Adam had pushed his mother was a question that would likely never be answered. Was it curiosity? An accident? A small grudge that had felt monumental in the moment?

From his journal entries, I believed Reverend Duffy had known what Adam had done, too, and it had changed him forever. Rather than expose his son, the reverend had kept him under watch at the Aerie. The reverend's formerly upbeat view of life had now been poisoned, and his craving for the misdeeds of others was a way to try to understand the evil in his own home.

The Aerie had burned to the ground in the wildfire and left Marlin Hill a scorched plat of forest at the end of the highway. The good news was that Lucy would have a fat insurance check to help her as she reestablished herself on the East Coast and awaited the baby with family. The revelation that her own brother-in-law had killed her husband had come as a horrific shock that only family and time could soothe.

As for Ellie, she was grounded and would be for a while. At her mother's insistence, she'd written notes of apology to everyone who'd received a poison-pen letter. These letters, people were glad to see, were written by hand. There would be no majorette camp for Ellie this summer. Not only that, her parents had arranged with the high school for her to assist the band leader in teaching baton twirling when school resumed. She'd be paid a stipend that was to go directly to people affected by the wildfire. Buffy and Thor, too, now had to run each of their money-making enterprises by Patty.

Dad wandered to Montgomery to talk philosophy. I found Mom alone at the edge of the patio, taking in the scene.

"What do you see?" I asked her.

She understood. "It will all be fine. This is an amazingly resilient little community."

I hesitated before my next question. I was afraid of her response but had to know. "Do you—do you see anything about Sam and me?" I'd kept calling him, but his phone rang and rang without even dropping into voicemail. Big House remained dark. Even from an assignment across the country he would have called—wouldn't he?

Worry tightened her brow. "I've tried. I haven't wanted to say anything."

"Because . . . ?" Dread bloomed in my chest. "It isn't good, is it?"

She looped an arm around me, and I swiveled to turn it into a hug. "It's not that," she said. "I don't see anything. At all. I try, and it's as if something is blocking me. I can't get even a hint."

"He hasn't called."

The fire crackled. Wilfredians let out a cheer as the last letter hit the fire.

"Josie, there's bad magic in the air. I don't know where it's coming from or what it's about, but things aren't as they seem. Sam loves you. I know that. However, something wants to keep you apart. Why and how, I have no idea." She looked into the distance, then at me. "There's one more thing. Your letter. We never did discover who sent it to you."

Mom was right. Despite the warm night, my skin prickled. I drew a deep breath and tried again. "Will it be okay? Can you at least tell me that?"

Beyond the café, from deep in the meadow, the chirping of crickets arose in the dusk. To me, their songs repeated *don't know, don't know, don't know*. My hand involuntarily rose to flatten against my chest.

"I hope so, honey. I sure hope so." She rested fingers on my forearm. "You're a strong woman. You'll see it through."

Visit our website at
KensingtonBooks.com
to sign up for our newsletters, read
more from your favorite authors, see
books by series, view reading group
guides, and more!

BOOK CLUB
BETWEEN THE CHAPTERS

Become a Part of Our
Between the Chapters Book Club
Community and Join the Conversation

Betweenthechapters.net

Submit your book review for a chance to win exclusive
Between the Chapters swag you can't get anywhere else!
https://www.kensingtonbooks.com/pages/review/